The No Dill Zone

A Spicetown Mystery

Sheri Richey

For further information, contact the publisher: Amazon Publishing.

ISBN: 979-8559061658

Cover art by Mariah Sinclair

Spicetown Mysteries

Welcome to Spicetown

A Bell in the Garden

Spilling the Spice

Blue Collar Bluff

A Tough Nut to Crack

Chicory is Trickery

The No Dill Zone

Romance by Sheri Richey:

The Eden Hall Series:

Finding Eden

Saving Eden

Healing Eden

Protecting Eden

Completing Eden

∾

Willow Wood

Knight Events

CHAPTER ONE

Spicetown Police Chief Conrad Harris leaned forward in his chair and propped his elbow on his desk while he waited for Officer Kimball to escort his visitor to his office.

"Good morning, Chief." Harvey Salzman scrunched his shoulders up and gave a feeble wave. "I know you're busy and I'm sorry about this, but I just need to talk to you about what's going on down Dill Seed Drive."

Harvey Salzman, known to his friends as Saucy, was a kind-hearted senior citizen who always kept abreast of city events and promptly reported any shady characters.

"Morning, Saucy." Conrad motioned for him to take a seat and nodded his thanks to Officer Kimball. "Do you want some coffee?"

"No thanks, Chief. Hey, is that the new officer?" Saucy whispered with his hand cupped near his mouth. "Wowee! I bet the mayor was surprised you hired a woman. I heard she moved here all the way from Minnesota, and she was a police officer there, too. That's really great. Now you don't have to train or anything."

"Yes," Conrad nodded. "Her name is Gwen Kimball and she's an experienced officer."

"Were you looking for a woman? Or was she just the best qualified? I never even thought of it, but I guess they do that now, don't they?"

Conrad chuckled. "Yes, Saucy. Women have worked in law enforcement for many years now and they do an exceptionally good job. Usually, they are better target shooters than the men."

"Really! Why do you think that is? Huh? They see better or what?" Saucy glanced toward Conrad's office door.

"I don't know why, and no, I wasn't specifically looking for a female officer, but it's a big help to have one on board."

"Oh, yeah. I bet it is. You get a whole different perspective and such." Saucy bounced one foot on his toes to provide relief for his anxiety.

"Saucy, you said you needed to tell me about something?"

"Oh, yeah. Yeah, there's a ruckus going on down Dill Seed Drive. The sign burglar has struck again!" Saucy raised his index finger in the air. "Everybody was outside this morning pulling up signs and fussing. I think old Dean Teggers is going to sit up all night tonight so he can nail the culprit. He's having a vigil and if it does happen tonight, the rest of us will take turns."

"What exactly happened?" Conrad frowned at the thought of citizens staking out the street.

"Well, you know I told you that a bunch of people woke up to find Hobart Emery's election signs pulled up from their yard."

Conrad nodded.

"I already had a new one there that I told Hobart he could put up weeks ago, but today, my sign was gone and everyone down the street has Larry Langley signs in their yard, including me!"

Conrad stifled a smile. "And no one saw anything? I would think it would take some time to hammer one of those things in the ground. I can't believe no one saw this happening."

"Larry's signs are metal like a house For Sale sign. They're easier to push in the ground. Hobart has the old fashion kind. They're just stapled to a wooden stake."

"Larry has run for election many times so I guess it's worth investing in the high-quality stuff." Conrad shrugged.

"I ran outside this morning and pulled that thing out of my yard right away. That's when I saw everybody else had the same thing. We all started talking and made a decision that this has got to stop."

"Now, Saucy. You don't need to stay up all night. I can tell Wink to make sure he increases patrol down Sage Street and Dill Seed Drive."

"That's a good idea, Chief. If we catch 'em, we're going to need backup. What can we charge 'em with? Property damage?"

"Maybe trespassing?" Conrad shrugged. "If they remove your sign and take it, it's property theft."

"There you go!" Saucy punched the air. "That's what we need to do."

Conrad laughed at Saucy's enthusiasm, but he knew he would have to get this situation under control before the neighborhood took over. "Thanks for letting me know what's happening and I'll see what I can do."

"Thanks, Chief," Saucy said as he walked to Conrad's door. "I'm going to take a nap now, so I can stay up late tonight."

§

"Mayor?" Amanda Morgan stood timidly at Cora Mae's office door as Cora glanced up. "Larry Langley is here to see you."

Cora shrugged her shoulders and sat up straight in her chair. Her eyes were bleary from looking at spreadsheets and an interruption might not hurt. "That's fine, dear. Send him in."

"I told him you were busy." Amanda's eyebrows went up encouragingly, but there was no reason to avoid the inevitable.

"That's okay. I need a break anyway."

"Okay."

"Mayor, I'm sorry to interrupt." Councilman Langley entered Cora's office with his chin down. He had been less than professional in his recent visits and Cora had warned him not to return if he could not conduct himself appropriately.

"Have a seat."

"First, I'd like to apologize for my behavior the last time we talked. This has been a very emotional time for me, and I have let my frustrations get the better of me."

Cora Mae nodded. She wasn't ready to release him from his guilt.

"The reason I stopped by is to keep you in the loop about something troubling. I just talked to Ned and he advised me to bring the issue to you before the next board meeting."

Cora frowned. Ned Carey, the Spicetown City Attorney, usually gave her a warning phone call if something was afoot among the council members. She hadn't heard from him this morning. "You have a legal matter to bring before the board?"

"I do," Larry nodded. "I want to register my concerns regarding Hobart Emery's qualifications to run for City Council. Aside from the fact that most of the citizens know he only keeps a mailing address within the city limits and actually lives with a woman in Paxton, there are abundant rumors that his petition signatures were purchased by a marketing firm and are not authentic."

"You are going to need more than town gossip to bring this issue to the board." Cora Mae clasped her hands on her desk.

"I know and that's not what I plan to provide the council." Larry opened his jacket and pulled out folded pages and passed them to Cora. "The charter states that a candidate for council cannot have a beneficial interest in a city contract or provide a service to the city."

Cora Mae leaned back in her chair and raised her eyebrows. Aware of the prohibition, she could not imagine how Larry could link Hobart's farm outside the city limits to a city contract. "We aren't buying soybeans from him."

Larry huffed. "No, but we are buying rock from him. The street department has a contract with the Spicetown Rock Quarry."

"Hobart retired and sold his interest in that quarry several years ago."

"He receives regular monthly payments from the quarry to this day! He is still getting paid from profits made off the city of Spicetown!" Larry's volume began to rise, and Cora Mae leaned forward to glare at Larry with her schoolteacher focus.

"You need to take a deep breath." She was poised to throw him out of her office if he took one more wrong step.

"Sorry." Larry inhaled deeply and sat back in his chair.

"Now, it's very possible that Hobart receives a pension or an installment payment from some arrangement he made with the quarry when he retired. It would not indicate that he benefits in any way from the amount of income received by the quarry from the City or from any source. It is a payment due to him and it is a set amount. I don't think you have a valid argument toward disqualifying him from the council race, but you have my consent to bring the issue to the City Council if that is your wish."

"Thank you."

"However, you should know that council meetings are public record and unless you have clear and convincing facts, this action will most likely make you look as bad or worse than your opponent, so I would think long and hard about it before you do it."

"But people need to know!"

Cora waved her hands in front of her. "It's your decision. I just want you to look at all angles first. Personally, I wouldn't recommend it, not without real evidence. You're making a suggestion of impropriety without any proof or knowledge of the source or intent of those monthly payments. It's not convincing evidence and I think it's premature to bring it the council right now."

"Ned said that once the allegation was made, it would be investigated. Hobart needs to answer to-\-"

"To the charges you're trying to bring up?" Cora Mae shook her head. "Larry, you're running against Hobart. No one is going to accept these allegations from you as having credibility."

"So, what do you suggest?" Larry threw his hands up in the air.

"Ask him." Cora Mae smirked. "You have a town hall meeting coming up. Ask him what his connection is, and the audience can decide. It's still a risk. He might come out looking better than you, but if you feel that strongly that this issue needs to be addressed, do it in a public forum."

"I hadn't thought of that." Larry hummed quietly. "Thank you, Mayor. I won't take up any more of your time." Rising from his chair, he left swiftly without a goodbye.

"Have a good day, Larry," Cora called out in a high voice as she saw his back pass through Amanda's outer office door. "Ugh." The man had no manners.

Conrad sauntered into Cora's office grinning. "You and Larry hanging out now?"

Cora giggled and waived her hand at Conrad.

"Did he act right this time?"

"It took effort and a wee bit of scolding, but he kept it together this time. The man is going to have a nervous breakdown."

"Hasn't he ever had an opponent before? He's been a council member as long as I've been in Spicetown. Hasn't anyone challenged his seat?"

Conrad dropped down in the chair facing Cora's desk.

"Not in a long time. I think his problem is that he feels vulnerable this time."

"Is Hobart Emery a popular guy? I don't know much about him."

"I don't even think it's about Hobart. I think it's because of what Larry's been through the last few years with his daughter and the bad press he got over his behavior right before Christmas when she was arrested. Some folks in town feel like he's grown a bit too big for his britches and a new face might be a good option."

"Oh, so it's all over his fear of losing," Conrad said with a stern nod. "He's become a career politician and he won't know what to do with himself."

"With a little bit of ego thrown in." Cora Mae chuckled. "He was just in here warning me that he's going to ask the council to disqualify Hobart from running for City Council because he draws a pension from the rock quarry."

"Huh?" Conrad shook his head.

"The City has a contract with the quarry. He thinks that violates the provisions of eligibility to run for council. It's true that he couldn't run if he was still working there or owned the business."

"So, it's a good try, but it's not going to work for him."

"No, but he can make a fuss about it if he wants. I warned him it might make him look bad. He can't see the situation clearly."

"Fighting on the street with your opponent doesn't make you look good either. That stunt he pulled at the parade was embarrassing! Fighting with Hobart over where his car was going to be placed in the parade and screaming at him in front of everyone..." Conrad dropped his head and sighed. "Shameful."

"I know." Cora leaned back in her chair. "It's been a long day. I'll be glad when this election is over."

"The next election in two years will be your turn to be the candidate. I hope Larry doesn't try to run against you!"

"Believe me, I've been thinking about that long and hard. I'm too old for this nonsense." Cora pushed her desk chair back and opened her desk drawer.

"No more election talk. Let's talk dinner!"

CHAPTER TWO

Arlene Emery spread her new quilt out over the top of the double bed in her guest room and took a picture with her phone.

"What are you up to in here?" Hobart stepped in the room and looked at the bed.

"What do you think?" Arlene squirmed with excitement. “Do you like it?"

"I see Beulah's curtains in there." Hobart pointed to the star formations in the quilt. "The kitchen ones and the bedroom curtains are right there."

"Yes, and the edging is all in the living room drapes. Do you think she'll like it?"

"It's real pretty, honey." Hobart squeezed his wife's shoulders. "I'm sure she'll love it."

"Oh, I hope so. I hope she recognizes them."

"Now, I can't promise that. Sometimes she doesn't know me, and I've been around a might longer than those curtains."

Arlene laughed. "I understand. I just thought it might bring her a little piece of home."

"What's the pictures for?"

"Oh, Peggy from the Carom Seed Craft Corner has the community center quilting event this weekend and I'm going to take it down there just for show. She wants some samples to hang and I told her I'd just finished one."

"Are you going to be down there all weekend?"

"Oh, no. Just a bit on Saturday, I think. I didn't offer to sit up there with her, but I will want to go down and see everyone else's work."

"Good. I'm taking a day off on Sunday. I've driven to Paxton every day for over a month now and I told Beulah I wouldn't be there Sunday. I need a day of rest."

"A lot of people drive that every day to work, but I would go crazy if I had to do that."

"I'll start back on Monday because I've got to meet the flooring people at her house. I'm just not sure my visiting her every day is a good thing. She's going to start counting on that every day and I can't keep that up. Slowly, I'd like to get her comfortable with just a weekly visit."

"You have the town hall meeting tomorrow night. Are you up to it?"

Hobart shook his head. "I guess so. I just hope Larry can be cordial. I never thought this would turn into such a brawl every time I get near him. I really didn't expect it to upset him so much. He's been on the council for twenty years and he's had some troubles lately. I wasn't even sure he was going to run again."

"I wish you hadn't even done it. I can't believe how people act! It's not just Larry. The ladies at the beauty shop were catty about it and I feel like people around me are whispering every time I go out to shop."

"I'm sorry, honey. I didn't mean to bring all this trouble. If he had been a decent guy, I would have just stepped aside, but the way he's acted, he doesn't deserve the job."

"Oh, I agree. I want to see you win now that you're in it. I just don't think I'm cut out for politics."

Hobart chuckled. "Maybe I'm not either. I went down to the bank yesterday and Gary waited on me. He said Larry had been in asking questions about me to one of the other tellers."

"About your bank accounts?" Arlene gasped.

"Yes," Hobart nodded. "I think he feels like as a council member he has superpowers above the law and people are just supposed to give him what he wants. He got short with the teller when she wouldn't answer his questions, so Gary stepped over there to help send him on his way. He's got a lot of nerve."

"I'll say!" Arlene huffed.

"It'll all be over soon." Hobart patted Arlene's back.

§

"Joyce!" Bert Miller stormed into his house after going down to the mailbox to collect the mail and waved the letter in his hand. "You're not going to believe this." Bert shook the letter at his wife when she walked into the kitchen.

"What's happened? Who is the letter from?" Joyce pulled open the refrigerator and removed a pitcher of tea.

"Miriam Landry. I can't believe that woman. I knew better, but I tried to trust her for once. The letter says we are invited to a meeting about forming a homeowners association on Lavender Lane."

"What? She promised there wouldn't be one." Joyce poured a glass of tea for each of them and carried them to the table. "We talked about this."

"I know and she mentions that in here. It says that some owners are interested in forming an HOA and it is up to the owners to decide. It's not her idea at all." Bert rolled his eyes. "I'm not living under Miriam's rule. If that happens, I'm putting the house up for sale!"

"Bert! We can't do that." Joyce loved her new house.

"Sure, we can."

"It won't make any difference to Miriam if we stay or leave. She's already gotten our money for the lot."

"That's true." Bert growled with frustration.

"Don't worry, honey. She can't even vote. She doesn't live out here." Joyce patted his hand.

"She threatens and intimidates people though. I've watched her do it for years. Every business owner in town has had her harassing them at one time or another. Now she's going to start harassing people in their homes."

"Don't overreact. We'll go to the meeting and see what it's about first."

"No good can come of this." Bert pointed his finger at Joyce. "I'm telling you."

"What would motivate her to be involved in this?" Joyce sat back and raised her eyes in thought. "She wouldn't be involved unless she benefited. Perhaps she's planning on building out here."

"That's another promise broken if she is. I asked her when we bought this lot and she told me then that she would not be moving out here."

"She could have changed her mind. The lots have stopped selling and she's still holding a lot of property."

"Having an HOA isn't going to help her sell these lots." Bert propped his chin in his hand. "She's up to something."

"Perhaps we need to have an informal owner's meeting before the actual HOA meeting," Joyce said with a wry smile. "Why don't we try to get everyone together at our house? Call it a block party!"

"Good idea! I'll get the grill out and we'll have everyone for lunch Saturday. Maybe we can get to the bottom of this!"

Joyce squeezed Bert's hand and smiled. "It'll be fun." She loved a party.

§

"We got 'em, Chief!" Saucy flew into Conrad's office the next morning before Conrad could even start his coffee maker. "We got a license plate number. It's a white truck and there's a woman in it."

"Slow down, Saucy. Take a deep breath and sit down. Would you like some coffee?"

"No, thanks, Chief. I'm sorry it's early, but I've been waiting since four o'clock."

Conrad sat down at his desk and glanced at the coffee pot that was still dripping. "Okay, so start from the beginning."

"Last evening, I walked down to talk to Dean Teggers. We worked out a schedule that he would sit up until two o'clock and then I would get up and take over. That way we both got some sleep."

Conrad nodded.

"Me and Zippy parked ourselves on the couch. I knew if I dozed off and something happened, Zippy would wake me up."

"Zippy is your dog?"

"Yeah. Yeah, I didn't fall asleep though. Zippy did."

Conrad laughed as he got up to make himself that vital first cup of chicory for the day. "Okay. What happened next?"

"I first saw the truck at Carol's house on the corner of Sage Street. The truck stopped and a woman got out. I couldn't tell much at that distance, except she has a slim build, kind of tall. She pulled up Hobart's sign, put it in the back of her truck and planted Larry Langley's sign right in the middle of the yard." Saucy swung his arm up in the air. "Big as you please!"

"She didn't see you?" Conrad returned to his desk and grabbed a small notepad.

"Nope and I didn't make a peep. Zippy would have been barking if he'd stayed awake, but I just watched her. It took everything I had to not run out there when she came to my house, but I knew I had to let her move on by so I could see the plate. After I got it, I turned on my porch light and she took off."

"Let me see it." Conrad reached for the paper in Saucy's hand. "So, you didn't know her? Even when she got to your yard, she didn't look familiar?"

"No, and all I could really tell is she's slim and young, maybe twenty." Saucy shrugged. "I'm guessing. I think everyone looks twelve nowadays, so I'm not a good judge. She had a hat on so I couldn't see her hair color, but her coat was red or purple. Hard to be sure under the streetlights."

"Excellent work, Saucy! I'll run this plate and pay her a visit. Maybe we can get those signs back for you."

"But aren't you going to tell me who she is?" Saucy leaned forward in his chair with a pout forming.

"I'll let you know once I locate her. She may not be the owner of the truck. Being young like that, it might be her parent's truck or a friend's. Just let me look into it first."

"Oh, okay. At least she only got four signs off of Dill Seed Drive this time, but she'll probably be back tonight unless you find her today."

"You tell Dean Teggers that we've got this handled now. No need for anybody to lose any more sleep. Okay?"

"I'll tell him." Saucy shuffled to the door looking like the inflatable tube dancer in front of the used car lot when someone cuts off the air.

"I'll make sure and tell the mayor. She's been worried about these election hi-jinks. She'll be very pleased that you cracked the case."

Saucy's face lit up. He always sought the approval of the mayor. "It's deplorable. Elections are a respectable function of history and the way this one is being handled is very disappointing. Poor sportsmanship!"

"We may find out that this is nothing more than a prank. I don't expect anybody will change their vote because of it."

Saucy turned around at the door and wrinkled his brow. "They might if they find out Larry Langley is behind it."

CHAPTER THREE

The next morning, Conrad pulled open the front door to the Fennel Street Bakery and waved to his coffee group tucked away in the corner. With his hot chicory in his travel mug, he looked at the pastries on display.

"Morning, Chief. What can I get you?" Vicki Garwin was the owner of the Fennel Street Bakery and it had been her business that had started the idea long ago of naming the town retail establishments with spices. Vicki hadn't named her bakery with the intention of using a spice name. It was the name of the main street, but it was the spark that launched the town's tradition. With her white hair tied up in a bun, she grabbed a plate and waited for Conrad's decision.

"I think I want to try something different today. What do you suggest?"

"Hmm, I have turnovers. Have you ever tried them?" Vickie pointed through the glass at triangular shaped pastries oozing with fruit. "I have lemon blueberry and cherry cheesecake."

Conrad growled. "I'll try the blueberry."

Vicki nodded and slid open the case to plate the pastry and Conrad followed her to the cash register. "Are you going to the town hall meeting tonight?"

"Yeah, I plan to be there. You?"

"Yes." Vickie leaned forward and lowered her voice. "I think you better bring a few other officers along with you in case there's trouble."

Conrad's eyebrows shot up. "You're expecting trouble?"

"I expect trouble anywhere Larry Langley goes! I had to ask him to leave this morning because he started an argument in here with some of my patrons. What's gotten into him?"

"He's been a little uptight lately." Conrad picked up his plate and fork. "I'm sure everything will be okay this evening."

"Hmm," Vickie looked skeptical. "If he can't handle the election, how is he going to handle it when he loses?"

Conrad forced a smile and drifted away from the counter, searching the room for his morning gang. Ned Carey, the city attorney, was seated between Ted Parish, the owner of Chervil Drugs, and Dr. Scott Jeffers, but Conrad could tell a fourth person had already taken his usual seat.

"Morning, Chief." Bert Miller raised his hand in greeting when Conrad appeared. Bert had been a regular morning coffee drinker with the group in the past, but last spring he had stopped showing up to join them.

"Morning, Bert. You haven't joined us for months now. I thought since you moved out to that fancy subdivision, you were too good for us old city guys." Conrad chuckled as he found a spot to place his plate on the table and went to grab an empty chair.

"I know, but now that the house is finished and we're all moved in, I'm getting things back to normal." When Bert and his wife began the process of building a new home, he had spent long hours fixing up his prior home for resale and he had lacked the energy and time for camaraderie.

"Did you sell your house?" Ned Carey asked.

"Not yet. It's listed with Red Pepper Realty, and they've shown it some, but no offers yet. The way things are going, I may be moving back into it."

"What?" Ted Parish jerked back in his seat. "Why in the world would you want to do that? You don't like it out there?"

"I did, but now Miriam is meddling and I'm getting concerned." Bert looked to his left and his right. "She promised me when I bought that lot, that she was not moving out there, and she wouldn't interfere. Now she's mailing out notices of a meeting to talk about forming a homeowners association. I told her from the beginning that I didn't want to buy there if that was being considered."

Ted dabbed a napkin across his mouth. "They've got one of those things next door at the subdivision on Cumin Court. She's always competing with them. That's probably why she wants it."

"Is she moving out there?" Ned Carey scowled. "If she's not a homeowner, she's got no business getting involved in a homeowners association."

"She said she was just organizing the meeting. She claims that some of the owners are interested. I don't believe her."

"When is the meeting?" Conrad brushed the crumbs of sugar from his fingertips.

"Monday evening," Bert said. "But Joyce and I have invited everyone to come over this weekend for a cookout and I'm going to find out what they know."

"Good idea." Ted pointed at Bert. "Did you talk to Earl Lester next door to you yet? I've known Earl since we were kids and I know he won't vote for such nonsense. He doesn't have a stomach for Miriam's shenanigans either."

"I talked to Earl and you're right. We agree that we didn't sign up for this and he's with me."

"Would you really move back to your old house and sell this new house?" Ned Carey shook his head. "I'd think Joyce would have your head for that."

Bert laughed. "She's not inclined to move back, but I know from experience that if you let Miriam in your life, your life is miserable. The woman is a poison. I'm not going to live under her rule. Can you imagine what kind of power base she could create? She'd tell me where I could put my mailbox, what I could plant in my front yard, when I can cut a tree down, and I can just see her stopping by to tell me to mow my yard. I'm not living like that!"

Conrad nodded. He hesitated to get involved in these emotional exchanges, however, he saw the same future that Bert imagined.

"Well, I better be getting back home. Joyce will be looking for me."

"Make sure you come by on Tuesday and tell us how it went." Ted held up his coffee cup for a refill from Vicki as she passed by the table.

Bert nodded and waved as he slipped out the front door.

§

Dorothy Parish yanked open the Carom Seed Craft Corner shop door, and the bells overhead jingled. The store was empty, and Dorothy began to walk toward the back to look for the owner, Peggy Cochran. "Yoo-Hoo, Peggy are you back there?" Dorothy glanced at her watch. She only had about ten minutes before she needed to open the Caraway Cafe. "Peggy! Where are you?" Dorothy advanced into the employee only area when she heard the back door slam followed by a crash. "Peggy?"

"Ugh. Oh, Dot I've made a mess. I'm sorry I didn't hear you. I was loading some things in my car around back. It's usually pretty quiet first thing in the morning and I've got a lot of supplies to take over to the community center to get ready for the weekend."

"Exactly what I came to talk to you about! Here, let me help you stack these back up." Peggy had white plastic totes stacked too highly and they had taken a tumble.

"At least they didn't spill open." Peggy sighed. "I don't know why I thought these events at the community center were such a good idea. I had no idea how much work they were going to be."

"But they're good for business, aren't they?"

"Yes. I think so. I do feel like I've had more customers since this started, but the time I've given to it is beginning to wear on me."

"You need a vacation!" Dorothy gave Peggy a playful punch in the arm. "You just need to hang in there until the holidays are over, then take some time off."

Peggy forced a smile. "Actually, I've been giving some thought to more than that. I'm thinking about closing next spring. I don't have any reliable help. I can't take a vacation and I don't know if I can keep struggling to do everything."

"Oh, Peggy. I had no idea. I'm sure we can find you someone. If you could get someone knowledgeable in here, someone who could help customers out with their projects, even a couple of part-timers, it would make all the difference."

"Yes, and I've tried, but I've always been disappointed. Were you wanting to come help me with the community center quilt show this weekend?"

Dorothy laughed. "You know I wouldn't be any help. I can't tie two pieces of string together!"

Peggy laughed. "I know."

"Actually, I was wanting to know if I could hold a meeting in the community center after your event closes. I don't think my restaurant will hold everybody."

"The Merchants Association meeting?"

"Yes. Since I put the notice in the paper, I've heard from over thirty people and they all want to come. I think I've got to move this to a bigger place. Cora Mae told me that you were closing to the public at six o'clock, so I thought maybe we could use the area. Will there be room?"

"Oh, yeah. There will be tables set up around the room, but we only take about half of the space. You can set up chairs on the other side and it won't interfere at all."

"Okay, good. I'm going to need your help. I'll be over there Saturday before you close up."

§

Cora Mae stirred sugar into her hot tea and took a deep breath. "I ate too much tonight. Jo, the Stromboli was excellent."

Jo Anne Biglioni smiled as she picked up Conrad's plate. "Thank you. Did you get enough, Chief?"

"Mercy!" Conrad patted his stomach. "Too much, but it was good."

"Well, I'm glad you both liked it. I think it was better with the sausage and we may just make it a regular menu item."

"Wonderful," Cora said. The Old Thyme Italian Restaurant was a regular stop for Cora and Conrad. Jo Anne's father, Joe Biglioni, had been the one to start the challenge in town. He had taken what Vicki had unintentionally started with her Fennel Street Bakery and encouraged the rest of the town to incorporate spice names into their businesses. Joe had been very influential during those early years when Cora's husband, Bing, had been mayor. He had always supported Bing and encouraged his ideas of individualism and growth for Spicetown. When Bing passed away and Cora Mae became mayor, she used that unique naming strategy to promote tourism for the small town.

"I hope you both enjoy the town hall event. I'm glad I have to work tonight. It gives me a good excuse not to go." Jo Anne chuckled. "I'm not much for politics."

"I can't say that it's my favorite thing either," Cora said. "I do think it's important to get the right people on the city council though."

"Are these guys the right people?" Jo raised her eyebrows in question.

"Larry's been doing it for years, but I don't know much about Hobart's perspective. I've known Hobart for a long time, but we never talked about what his vision for Spicetown is, so I can't really say. Maybe the town hall meetings will help answer those questions for me. I was trying to get Jimmy Kole to run this time, but I couldn't talk him into it."

Conrad laughed. "Jimmy's a smart boy."

"If you don't like either of these guys, I guess you can always write in Jimmy's name." Jo Anne held out her hands and shrugged.

"Now, that's a thought," Cora said as Jo moved to the next table. "I might just have to do that."

CHAPTER FOUR

Cora and Conrad arrived at the meeting early and as expected, Cora Mae took off into the crowd to visit with everyone as Conrad stood near the back wall by the door. Looking over everyone's head, he spotted Wink Hobson standing at the side door and Officer Darren Hudson near the stage. Before he could duck into the lobby, Harvey Salzman began waving his arm in the air to get Conrad's attention, and he waited while Saucy made his way over to the door.

"Chief! So glad I spotted you. Do you have anything you can share with me? Do you know who owns the truck?"

"I do, Saucy, but it's not a young woman."

"So, what does that mean? What happens next?"

The incoming crowd jostled them both around and they had to move to the side. "The owner doesn't live in Spicetown, so I asked the Sheriff's office to make contact with the owner and see who was using their truck."

"Oh, okay." Saucy nodded and frowned. "Then you'll go pick them up?"

"Then I'll try to locate them and talk to them."

"Dean says he's sitting up tonight. He thinks she'll be back."

"You don't need to do that. We're watching your street. You've done all you can do at this point."

"Saucy, you better find a seat," Cora Mae said when she walked up. "I see Paulie Childers walking up on stage. It's about time to start."

"Oh, I've got a good seat up front. I'll see you two later."

"Thank you." Conrad nodded to Cora.

"Is he trying to get you to arrest his sign thief?" Cora smiled.

"Yes, and I'm going to ask Hobart about it if I get a chance tonight. It seems strange to me that he hasn't come to me about it. I know he knows. Saucy's talked to him and the other neighbors have contacted him to get replacement signs when they are taken from their yard. It's got to be costing him money and time."

"Hobart is pretty easy-going. He may just see it as futile. Larry's thrown a lot at him the last few months and he seems to take it all in stride." Cora returned a wave to someone in the crowd.

"I hope that holds out tonight."

Cora chuckled and turned to find a seat when Paulie Childers, a reporter for the Spicetown Star, took the stage and tested the microphone.

"Good evening, everyone. My name is Paulie Childers, and I want to welcome you to our event tonight. The Spicetown Star is sponsoring this town hall meeting platform to provide the citizens of Spicetown the opportunity to hear a little bit more from each of our City Council candidates. The election is right around the corner, so if you still have questions, tonight is the night for you to get those answered."

Paulie smiled through the light applause. "I will be your moderator tonight and we will open with each candidate giving us an introduction first, then I have a few questions submitted by readers that I will ask each candidate. They will each have another opportunity at the end to speak to you."

Paulie looked left and right, then pulled the microphone from its stand. "On your right is Councilman Larry Langley." The applause was a bit lackluster, so Paulie turned to Hobart. "And on your left is candidate Hobart Emery. Councilman Langley won the coin toss and has chosen to address you first during the opening and last at closing. Councilman Langley..."

Paulie scurried from the stage and put the microphone in his stand on a desk facing the stage and nodded at Larry to begin. The crowd fidgeted and mumbled as Larry straightened his shoulders.

"I want to welcome all of you this evening to our meeting and thank the Spicetown Star for giving me this opportunity to talk with each of you. My name is Larry Langley, but I don't think I need to tell any of you this. I look out at this sea of faces and I think I can put a name to every face. You already know me. I have served you and the city of Spicetown for almost twenty years, and my record speaks for itself. What I think we need to focus on tonight is my opponent." Larry swept his arm out to his side. "I don't think any of you really know Mr. Emery, and to make an informed decision on election day you should know who you're voting for. Mr. Emery may receive mail in Spicetown, but his life is elsewhere. His days are spent on his farm or traveling daily to Paxton. I am here every day. Being your councilman is my main priority in life. My attention is always focused on city hall. I'm not running a business, running a farm, and running to Paxton. I'm here for you, and I hope you will support me in my continued goals to keep the city of Spicetown running smoothly. Thank you."

Larry nodded as the crowd politely applauded and Paulie tapped the microphone. "Thank you, Councilman Langley. Mr. Emery, you may begin."

"Well, Larry's right. You all don't know me as a politician, but I do see some familiar faces out there that I'd call a friend. For those who don't know me, my name is Hobart Emery, and my wife is Arlene." Hobart pointed to his wife in the front row, and she stood up to turn and wave to the crowd bashfully.

"I've not been overly involved in politics over the years. I was busy. I owned a business, the Spicetown Rock Quarry, tried to farm some soybeans, and took care of my family. Not a lot of time was left for politicking. I'm retired from the rock business now and my little farm is running smoothly. My regular trips to Paxton have been to help take care of my sister who is suffering from dementia, but I've got her set up in a safe environment now. She's getting the right care, so I expect those regular trips won't be so frequent. I'm still going to visit her every weekend and keep an eye on her. Family comes first to me and I hope all of you share that same oath. What it comes down to is this: I think I've got my family taken care of now and I'd like to help you take care of yours."

The roar of applause startled Paulie and he held up his hand for quiet as Larry scowled. "Please hold your applause."

"I think Spicetown can use someone with an open mind, someone who wants to see the town grow, and maybe someone who isn't all eaten up with politics." The applause began again despite Paulie's flailing arms. "That's all. Thank you."

Paulie tapped the microphone causing a loud thud and reminded everyone again that applause was not appropriate until the end. "Thank you, both. Gentlemen, the first question goes to Councilman Langley."

The audience quieted to a murmur and Larry stepped up to his podium.

"Councilman Langley, recently the City Council received a proposal from Buddy Burger, a fast-food franchise in Paxton. Please tell us whether or not you are in favor of this type of expansion and why."

Larry cleared his throat. "I'm very familiar with this proposal and have examined many like it over the years. There are elements that have to be developed and considered before a decision can be made. An examination of pros and cons is needed; the council has to look at every angle. Will this business be prosperous here? Does the city benefit from allowing this new business to join us? I realize there are some that shy away from change, but I feel we cannot continue to fight the future. We cannot compete for tax revenue when we do not offer the businesses that our citizens want and need."

"Mr. Emery?"

"Sorry, Larry, but I'm against it. Burger Buddy? Really? Not only is it a low rent establishment, the food is awful."

The audience laughed, clapped, and giggled through Paulie's objections. "Please!"

"I am open to growth, positive growth, adding new assets to our town, but not everything that is new is good. I will be voting no on that proposal."

Hobart nodded curtly to Paulie to indicate his response was complete.

"Thank you, Mr. Emery. The next question is for you." Paulie held up his note cards. "Some of the citizens of Spicetown--"

"You don't have any idea how a new business impacts a town. You don't know about taxing base, commercial zones, liability risks," Larry shouted. "You don't have a clue what's involved in making a decision of that importance."

Hobart looked out into the audience and smirked, but Paulie jumped from his chair. "Councilman, please. Do not speak out of turn. You will get your opportunity to respond."

Larry huffed.

"My apologies, Mr. Emery," Paulie said as he sat back down to read his next card again. "Some of the citizens of Spicetown are struggling in the current economy. What help do you think the City Council could or should offer to its citizens?"

"I feel that City Hall should be a resource to the community, not just a place to pay your water bill. We could do more. We should network with the county and neighboring small towns to find help. We should establish a program here, right here in Spicetown, to help the needy--"

"Just throw money at everybody. Is that what you think? You think the city can just support everybody in it? That just shows what a buffoon you are, Hobart." Larry continued to rant and point his finger at Hobart, but only the front row could hear him because Paulie had clicked off his microphone. The crowd began to squirm and talk among themselves as the buzz rose in the room. A few hecklers could be heard shouting at Larry and then some people began to rise from their seats to leave.

Conrad's foreboding instincts led him down the middle aisle toward the stage. He had witnessed several degrees of Larry's anger over the years and when his face was this shade of red, it usually meant his judgment was impaired. As he drew closer, he could hear Larry's threatening words, yet Hobart showed no response. Pausing at the front edge of the stage, he turned left and walked toward Paulie and Hobart.

Cora jumped up from her aisle seat and followed Conrad but turned right and stood glaring at Larry. Her back was facing the audience, but she hoped her presence would give Larry some focus. She didn't want to embarrass him further, but she couldn't sit idle while he behaved so unprofessionally in front of the whole town.

"Paulie, do you want to shut this down?" Conrad glanced over at his officers standing on each side of the stage.

"Uh, well. I don't know, Chief. I, if Larry can't... Maybe a brief intermission would suffice. I don't know." Paulie was rattled. It was clear he had no plan for handling Larry's outburst, but the crowd was becoming more outspoken the longer Larry yelled. At least a dozen people were walking out.

Cora Mae put her hands on her hips, but Larry only had eyes for Hobart. Glancing at Conrad, she knew Paulie was hesitating.

When Conrad heard Larry's word choice further deteriorate, he barked at Paulie. "You need to shut this thing down now." Larry had a history of resorting to inappropriate behavior when enraged. He had taken his wrath out on Conrad a time or two.

"I'm sorry ladies and gentlemen," Paulie said as he grabbed the microphone and turned to the audience. "I'm afraid we will have to close out our evening prematurely. I hope you feel better acquainted with your council candidates, and I assure you that the Spicetown Star will do all we can to offer you additional information on both candidates between now and election time. We want to encourage everyone to exercise your right to vote, and please send any questions you have to the Spicetown Star. Have a good evening and drive safely."

Cora hadn't waited for Paulie's speech. She had hooked her hand in Larry's elbow and pulled him away from the podium until he was out of the audience's sight.

"Larry!" Cora tempered her yell to a raspy whisper. "What are you doing? What has gotten into you? You have got to get a hold of yourself."

Larry's head dropped and he took a deep breath. "I know Cora. That was bad. I just can't think straight when he says stupid things like that! He doesn't have any idea how to be a councilman. How can he even think about running against me?"

"Larry, did you know how to be a councilman when you were first elected?"

Larry shrugged. "I guess not."

"I really think you need to seriously consider some counseling or some healthy outlet for managing your anger. It's destroying your career. It may have just lost you this election."

"No. I'll go apologize. It'll be all right."

Larry's wife, Doris, joined them with worry etched across her forehead. "Are you okay? Let's go home. Let's go out the back door."

"No, I need to go back out there and apologize."

"Larry, there's nobody out there to talk to. They've all gone home."

Cora squeezed Doris' arm and gave her a sympathetic nod but left the situation to Doris to handle. Walking across the stage, there were very few people still in the auditorium, and she joined Paulie at Hobart's podium.

"I'm sorry about all this, Mr. Emery. I was not prepared. I didn't even see it coming."

"No worries, Paulie. I'm happy to get home early. You come out Saturday and see me. I'll give you an interview to fill in the questions you didn't get an answer to tonight, if you'll give me the opportunity to give you my closing remarks."

"It's a deal."

"Good. I'll consider us square then." Hobart chuckled. "Madame Mayor." Hobart removed his cap and bowed toward Cora. "Sorry for the disturbance, but I just seem to bring out the worst in Larry."

"I've done it a time or two myself." Cora smiled. "But I'm not here to apologize for him. I just wanted to commend you on your response to his behavior. You handled yourself very well. Much appreciated."

"Thank you."

"Good luck, Hobart." Cora stepped down from the stage and caught Conrad's eye as he finished talking with Wink.

"Are you ready to go? Wink said he'd stick around and close up with Paulie. Is Larry gone?"

"I'm ready. Doris said she was taking him out the back door, so he should be gone. Hopefully, Hobart can walk safely to his car now."

CHAPTER FIVE

"Ted!" Hobart kicked the tractor tire. "Ted, what's this doing here? Was it left here all night?"

"Yes, sir. I guess Micky took off too quick last night." Ted Aldridge smiled. Hobart had hired Micky without even consulting him. He made one mistake after another, but Hobart always overlooked them.

"I'll talk to him."

"Anybody else and you'd fire them." Ted stared at Hobart in challenge, but Hobart looked away.

"I told you if we were going to switch this one field from soybeans to edamame successfully, we had a tight time frame. There's only a small window of harvest time and no room for mistakes. You should make sure the workers know that."

"So, it's my fault Micky did this? We're still short a man."

"Hiring and training is supposed to be your job." Hobart walked down the plant rows and checked his beans.

"Well, I can call Kevin back. He hasn't found a new job yet, but I know you don't like him either." Ted Aldridge jogged behind Hobart. His nephew,

Kevin Joiner, had worked for Hobart for most of the summer until Hobart fired him.

"This harvester is leased. These guys have got to understand that the equipment is to be taken care of. It's worth a lot more than they are."

"I understand, Hobart."

"Just get somebody in here. I don't care. I'm out of patience, Ted."

"I'll get on it."

"Did you get those signs delivered for me?"

"I did. Mr. Salzman told me there was a problem with signs disappearing, but we put them back up. Are you going to be around today? There is a guy that's been calling the office for you. I left you a message inside."

"Nope, I'm headed to the lake. It can wait until next week. I've got an appointment with some walleye. You can come along if you like."

§

Joyce Miller turned her car into her driveway and looked in the rear-view mirror. Felicia Ward lived across Lavender Lane from the Millers and she was on her porch wrangling a large wreath. Joyce hopped out of the car and skittered across the street. "Felicia."

"Oh, hi Joyce. How are you?" Felicia was stretched up onto her tiptoes trying to hook the wire circle on top of a wreath to a hook on her front door.

"I'm good. I just got home from the library and I saw you out here. Can I help you with that?"

Felicia grunted to get that extra half inch and exhaled. "Whew, no thank you. I think I've got it."

"It's beautiful. Did you make it?"

"I did! Peggy has some lovely things down at the Carom Seed Craft Corner and she helped me figure out what I needed. I'm happy with it."

"I've never tried making a wreath. Was it difficult?"

"Not at all. Peggy can show you how to get started. It was actually fun."

"Maybe I'll try it. I'm going down to the community center this weekend for the quilt demonstration. I'll ask her about it then. The reason I wanted to stop by is to check on tomorrow. Are you going to be able to make it over to our house for our cookout? Bert and I wanted to get everyone together and talk about the homeowners association issue before Miriam gets involved. I hope you can come."

"Yes, I'm sorry I haven't replied. I wanted to ask you if you invited Miriam."

"Heavens no! That's the whole reason we are doing this. We need to be prepared before we see Miriam. I'm hoping we will all be able to present a united front."

"Okay, then. Yes, we'll be there. I just didn't want to end up in a situation where she was coming, and it was going to be a big brawl. Eddie is not happy about the situation at all."

"Bert is equally upset. Our old house hasn't sold, and he's threatened to move back in it and sell our new house. I don't want that to happen."

"Did you invite Hobart Emery? You know he recently bought the lot at the end of the street. I assume he plans to build on it and he might want to be included in the meeting."

"No, I didn't know! I may see his wife, Arlene, tomorrow at the quilt show and I'll ask her or maybe Bert can give him a call today."

"I just made a Blueberry Buckle this afternoon. How about if I bring it over for dessert?"

"That sounds great. Thank you." Joyce walked down the porch steps.

"Call me if you need me to bring anything else?"

"I will." Joyce waved as she jogged back across Lavender Lane.

§

"Sergeant Cantrell!" Conrad rocked back in his office chair. He had just gotten his chicory and reached for his phone when it rang. "I was just planning to call you. Did you have any luck reaching Aaron Vaughn about his truck?"

"Hey, Chief. We did talk with Vaughn and he said his truck was at home all night. His wife drove it to work the next morning."

"Hmm, that doesn't sound right. Do you care if I take a try at it? Maybe try to talk to the wife?"

"No, not at all. If you want to drive over, you can take a deputy with you if you'd like."

"Did he happen to say where his wife works?" Conrad wrote himself a note on his desk pad.

"I wasn't the one that talked to him, but the report doesn't mention it."

"Okay, thanks for your help."

"Actually, I wasn't calling about that. We got a call this morning about a body in the lake. Pulled a dead guy out of Eagle Bay and the neighbors tell us he's from Spicetown."

"Boating accident?"

"Doesn't look like it." Sergeant Cantrell flipped through pages and Conrad could hear the paper rustle. "Hobart Emery. Know him?"

"Yeah, he's running for Spicetown City Council right now. I just saw him last night. Who found the body?"

"The call came from Hazel Linton on Eagle Bay Road, but she said her husband found him."

"Yeah, I know Hazel, too." She was perched in her front window most of the time and rarely missed any activity on Eagle Bay Road.

"The Sheriff thought you might want to weigh in on this. Come out to the scene and take a look. I've got officers out there now waiting on the coroner."

"Hobart's got a wife, Arlene."

"Officer Goldberg is doing the death notification and Detective Snell caught the case."

"I know Snell. I'll give him a call and see if he wants my help with interviews. Thanks for letting me know."

"Sure thing." Sergeant Cantrell disconnected and Conrad looked down at his phone puzzled by the hospitality. Sheriff Bobby Bell didn't usually show any. Maybe he was mellowing in his old age.

"Kimball," Conrad yelled as he grabbed his jacket. "You're riding with me."

CHAPTER SIX

After the deputies on the scene briefed Conrad and Officer Kimball, Conrad stepped up on the bank of the lake and wandered away from the group. Pulling out his phone, he dialed Cora's extension at City Hall.

"Hey, Connie."

"Good morning. Am I interrupting anything?"

"No. Not at all. Dorothy Parrish just left. She wants me to come down to the Merchants Association meeting Saturday evening and say a few words. She just left."

"Well, I thought I'd call and give you the bad news. Hobart Emery's body was found in the lake this morning. He's dead."

"Oh, no! How did it happen? Have you talked to Arlene yet?"

"Well, the sheriff's office is over there now. I just wanted to let you know."

"Was it accidental?"

"They don't know enough yet to say. I just got here."

"Well, I'll see if I can help Arlene. Keep me updated."

Conrad disconnected the call and turned around to find Officer Kimball behind him. "Calling the mayor."

"Oh," Gwen nodded. "You have to let her know?"

"Yeah, anytime there's a major incident she has to be notified. Plus, I know she's acquainted with the deceased and his wife."

"That's different," Gwen smirked. "We never had to do that in Minnesota."

Conrad smiled. "I doubt you had a mayor anything like we do."

Gwen chuckled. "That's true."

Conrad headed slowly back down the bank of the lake. "I think you'll find that Mayor Bingham is a big help to the police force, and she knows a little something about everyone in town. Before she was mayor, she taught fifth grade, so she had most of this town in her class at one time or the other."

Gwen nodded. "This doesn't look accidental. Did you see his head?"

Conrad nodded discreetly. They would talk further about this on the drive back to town.

"Chief Harris!"

Conrad reached out and shook Detective Snell's outstretched hand. "Detective Snell. It's been a long time."

"Good to see you, Chief. Sorry I'm a little late. I was in court this morning. Cantrell tells me that you know the victim."

"I do. Not well, but he's a bit of a public figure in Spicetown right now. He's a candidate for city council and running against an incumbent. It's been a high-profile race."

"Is this lake near his home? Or do you know why he would be out here?"

"He's a fisherman. I don't know if he was fishing today, but I've heard him talk about his interest. He lives in town, but I'd guess he has a boat out here. Just a little way down this bank there is a set of covered docks with lifts and you can rent the spaces. He may have a boat there."

"You know who handles the rentals?"

"I do."

"Would you mind getting that information for me? I mean if you--"

"Not at all. I'm happy to go with you when you interview the Lintons, if you'd like. The reporting party lives right up there over that hill." Conrad pointed up the bank. "Hazel called it in when her husband found the body. Hazel Linton has an eagle eye on Eagle Bay Road, so she should know if there had been anybody out in this area this morning."

"That's where I was headed next. Join me. Tell me about Hazel."

§

Cora Mae pulled her car into the Emery driveway, but there were no cars around. The two-car garage was closed, but a large black Labrador Retriever charged from the side of the house to greet her. Making eye contact with her greeter through her car window, she tried to assess the risk factors and then saw his tail wag in anticipation of company or lunch. She wasn't sure which. Easing her car door open slowly, she found a large wet nose nudging her hand in welcome.

"Well, hello there." Cora stroked the dog's head, and her words made his tail wag more vigorously. "Let's go see Arlene."

Arlene opened the front door as Cora Mae approached. "Arlene, I just came by to check on you. Is there anything I can do?" Cora Mae had lived through the loss of a spouse in a very public way. When her husband, George, died, he was the mayor of Spicetown, so it was a loss for everyone. Bing, as he was affectionately called, was a friend to everyone and Cora had to deal with grieving along with the rest of the town.

"Thank you, Cora. I think I'm still in shock." Arlene sniffed. "I just can't believe what they're telling me. The police just left."

"Would you like some company? Or is there someone I can call for you?"

"Please come in. I'd love it if you could stay a few minutes."

"Certainly." Cora followed Arlene into the living room and Cora slipped out of her coat.

"Can I get you anything? Some tea? I think I could use some tea. Let's go into the kitchen."

Cora sat at the kitchen table as Arlene ran water in her kettle.

"The police said they don't know anything yet. They said I have to wait until the coroner in Paxton looks at Hobart. What's going to happen now, Cora? I don't know if there's something I should be doing. They didn't tell me what to do. I just wait?" Arlene sat down at the kitchen table.

"You should know something in a few days. The coroner is Alice Warner, and she will look for clues to help the police figure out what happened and how he died. Sometimes she can't tell, but other times she finds out information that leads them to all the answers. It is a waiting game." Cora patted Arlene's hand.

"I know I sound crazy right now, but what difference does it really make for me?" Arlene placed her hand across her chest. "I need to know what to do right now. Hobart took care of the farm. He handled things for us, and I don't even know where to begin. It's the eeriest feeling to think that I'm all alone in the world so suddenly."

"It changes your life," Cora said, swallowing the knot in her throat. "I wish I could tell you that it will be better tomorrow, but it takes a lot of time, and it's different for everybody, but you will figure it out. You will know what to do and learn a new way to live, but you're not alone in the world. I'll always be here to help you and you have plenty of friends that will be there for you, too."

"It's such a sudden thing and I've never really fretted about it. I never planned for this."

"Well, I did, or I thought I did. With Bing's illness, his passing wasn't a surprise, but I don't think it softened the blow and I was still unprepared for the life changes that followed. No one can understand it until it happens to them."

Arlene jumped from her chair to grab the tea kettle and poured the hot water in cups. Arranging everything on the table neatly, Arlene returned to her seat. "I just don't feel like I can stay here tonight. I don't feel safe. I can't explain why, but I feel frightened and vulnerable. I called Peggy Cochran and talked to her before you arrived. I'm going to stay the night with her tonight. The craft store doesn't close until six o'clock, but then I'm going to go over to her house. I was going to help her tomorrow with the quilt show anyway."

"I think that's a good idea." Cora Mae stirred her tea. "Did you know Hobart had gone to the lake this morning or was that a surprise?"

"Oh, no. I knew he was going fishing. He left early and went to the farm first. He has to check on things there every day and then he was planning to fish. He has a boat docked at the Eagle Bay storage rental."

"It's pretty chilly outside. I don't think I'd want to be on the water." Cora shrugged. "But I'm not much of a fisherman. Bing took me a few times. He enjoyed it."

"Yeah, I feel the same. I never had any interest in it. I never learned to swim, so water makes me nervous." Arlene smiled weakly. "They told me he had a head injury. Did you know that?"

Cora nodded.

"I'm guessing he tripped and fell. He didn't have any health problems, at least nothing major. He goes to the doctor and gets a physical every year. We were blessed to not have any health scares so far. His father had a bad heart and Hobart always wanted to make sure..." Arlene sighed. "You just never think that an accident can take someone away in a minute." Arlene's voice was raspy with impending tears.

"Was Hobart fishing alone? Could there have been anybody else around that area?" Cora tried to picture the location Conrad described. Maybe if Arlene would refocus on the mechanics of the day, she could remain composed.

"He didn't mention anyone else. He usually went by himself."

"So, he was taking his boat out?"

Arlene nodded and dabbed a tissue at her cheek. "They told me he was close to the Linton's' house, but he usually parked his truck in the circle drive and walked down to the docks. I don't know why he was near the Linton's."

"Hmm, I don't know. I'm sure they'll check on the boat for you. Was Hobart in good spirits today? The town hall meeting was a little crazy last night."

"Oh, yes. He thought the meeting went well for him and Larry Langley didn't bother Hobart at all. He knew he got under Larry's skin and the funny thing is all he ever did was be nice to him."

"Not a lot of nice guys in politics." Cora smiled. "What does Hobart do at the farm? I don't know much about farming, but is that something you'll be able to continue?"

"Oh mercy. I don't know. Hobart has a good farm manager. Ted Aldridge runs the farm and I think he does a good job although he and Hobart did butt heads from time to time. I think Ted can take care of things until all the harvest is sold. Then I'll have to make some decisions." Arlene put her fingers to her temples and shook her head. "It's just so much, Cora. It's just too much to think about."

"I know," Cora said as she reached out for Arlene's hand. "You don't have to make any decisions today."

"Thank you for coming Cora. I know you need to get back to work."

"You know you can call me anytime. Right?"

"I know."

Cora stood with outstretched arms and Arlene hugged her before she walked her to the door.

§

After saying goodbye to Hazel Linton, Detective Snell walked to his car.

"If you don't mind, I'd like to go take a look at the boat dock." Conrad pointed down Eagle Bay Road. "I know Hobart had a boat in the rental sheds and I want to check and see if it's in there."

"Yeah, sure. That's a good idea. I'll go with you." Sam Snell locked his car and followed Conrad down the road with Officer Gwen Kimball close behind. Cora Mae had texted Conrad that she had visited Arlene and added that she had learned Hobart went to the lake to get his boat to go fishing.

"There's Hobart's truck." Conrad pointed to the end of the road. "That's usually where people park when they're going to drop a boat in the water or have one stored here. This road is a dead end."

"So, you think Hobart came down here to fish, went to the docks and fell in the water here? He could have drifted down to the Linton's house." Sam Snell nodded, but frowned. "Is there much fishing out here this time of year?"

"Not as much," Conrad said. "But there are always people fishing until the lake freezes."

"Real die hards, huh?" Sam chuckled and looked at Gwen. "I'm not a fisherman."

"I enjoy it. I just never get the time. Watch your head." Conrad parted the tree limbs and held them until Sam grabbed them before they snapped back. "It's a little overgrown right now. Here's the boat launch, and the docks are over here."

"Do you know which one was his?" Sam walked out on the first dock.

"I don't. Let me call his wife and ask." Conrad pulled out his phone and quickly dialed the number Cora had texted to him. "Mrs. Emery? This is Chief Harris... You have my condolences, Arlene...I hate to bother you, but I'm down at the boat dock and I just wondered if you knew which one belonged to Hobart? I wanted to check on-- Uh huh. Okay. I'll call you later. Thank you." Conrad slipped his phone in his pocket and pointed. "Number four."

Sam Snell walked back up the dock and followed Conrad.

"Not sure if she meant the fourth dock or the fourth boat, but she said it's a gray Triton."

Some of the boats were already lifted from the water and one dock was empty, but Arlene had been correct. There was a gray Triton boat in the fourth boat house.

"This it?" Sam followed Conrad, stepping gingerly around the edge of the dock.

"This is it, but we have a curious situation here." Conrad's chest heaved when he exhaled. "Those signs in the boat." Conrad pointed. "Those are his opponent's yard signs."

"What? Oh." Sam scowled and pulled out his camera to take a picture. "Hobart is running against Larry Langley?"

"Yes."

"But Cantrell told me you had somebody over here stealing yard signs. Maybe it was Hobart?"

"The signs that have been disappearing are Hobart's, not Larry's." Conrad walked to the other side of the dock to see if there was anything else in the boat unusual.

"Maybe Hobart decided to pay him back." Sam shrugged.

Conrad hummed. "Perhaps, but there's something we don't know. I think you need to talk to Larry Langley."

"You think he's a suspect? I mean if the coroner says this is a homicide. It could still be an accident."

Gwen shook her head.

"I guess we wait to see what Alice says." Conrad slapped the side of his leg. Alice Warner, the county coroner, would have an opinion the Sheriff's office would act on.

CHAPTER SEVEN

"Busy day, hmm?" Cora Mae slid into a booth at the Juniper Junction across from Conrad. He had arrived first and already had the menu open.

"Yes, a busy day, but at least it's Friday and this isn't my case. It belongs to the Sheriff's office."

"Maybe, but they need you and it looks like they are finally realizing that."

"Paulie Childers has been ringing my phone constantly today. He's freaked out about the election." Conrad chuckled. "I've enjoyed his frantic voice mails, but I can't help him. I can't make any statements about a Sheriff's office case. He needs to get his news from Paxton."

"I'm glad Arlene had somewhere to go tonight. She said she was afraid to stay home alone. I didn't directly ask her if Hobart had enemies. She wasn't in any shape yet for a question like that, but I wonder if those worries were because she knows something."

Conrad leaned forward and spoke softly. "Does she think he was murdered?"

"She didn't seem worried with whether it was murder or an accident. She was more concerned with being left alone. She's still struggling to deal with that and hasn't thought about the details yet."

"Hazel Linton was pretty rattled when we interviewed her. I've never seen her that way. I recommended we go back in a day or two and talk to her again, but I don't make the decisions. Hazel is usually very exact, incredibly detailed, but today she was nervous and distracted, just all over the place."

"Did you talk to Arlene?"

"I did. I called her briefly to find out which boat was Hobart's, but then I called back later in the afternoon, just to give her an update on where we are."

"Was Hobart's boat there?" Cora leaned back and paused when the waiter approached. Conrad quickly ordered his usual dish and Cora decided to try the Friday night Special, Chicken Biriyani.

Once the waiter was gone, Conrad looked around the room and leaned forward again. "His boat is in the dock, but I'm a little concerned with what we found in the boat."

Cora scrunched her shoulders up around her neck and leaned over the table to whisper. "What was in the boat?"

"Not a word now." Conrad shook his index finger at her.

Cora rolled her eyes. "Of course not."

"Larry's yard signs." Conrad leaned back in his seat and raised his eyebrows. "What do you make of that?"

"Oh, mercy," Cora said in a raspy whisper. "Do you think he was doing the same thing?"

Conrad shrugged. "Maybe."

"I don't see it." Cora Mae shook her head with a stubborn scowl on her face. "That doesn't fit, and he had no reason to do it. Maybe Larry was trying to set him up. I'd sooner believe that."

"I hadn't thought of that, but I think Larry used to keep a boat out there, too."

"Did you talk to Larry?" Cora took a sip from her water glass. "Where was he Friday morning?"

"Not my case, remember." Conrad chuckled. "I did suggest it, but Detective Snell is sitting on pause until the coroner makes her cause of death determination."

"What about all that hubbub you talk about all the time?" Cora put her fists at her waist and dropped her chin to imitate Conrad. "The first forty-eight hours are crucial. You need to identify witnesses and confirm location of all parties. Yak, yak yak."

Conrad chuckled.

"I've heard it a million times." Cora shrugged. "Does Detective Snell not know these things?"

"I guess he has a different method. He may have more pressing issues in Paxton. I did suggest that he talk to Larry, even offered to go along, and maybe we'll get there. I actually gave him a short list of people I thought he needed to contact and tried to explain the dynamics surrounding the election. He listened respectfully, but I don't think he plans to act on anything until Alice flags this case as a suspicious death. He has too much to do. There's too much crime in Paxton for him to dedicate time on a case that may be nothing. The scene wasn't even treated as a crime scene. I'm surprised they bothered to send a detective at all."

Cora Mae grunted. "You know what Alice is going to say. She's going to say he died of a head trauma or drowning, but neither one of those things will classify this case as murder or accidental. He's losing crucial time."

"It could have been a heart attack or aneurysm, some underlying heath issue that made him unconscious."

"Maybe," Cora said as her eyes darted around the restaurant. "Arlene told me Hobart was healthy. He had a yearly physical."

"Spouses sometimes keep secrets." Conrad raised his eyebrows up and down which made Cora smile.

"They do and that's something I could almost believe. Hobart might have had a health problem he kept from Arlene because he didn't want to worry her."

Conrad nodded. "Foul play is very hard to prove in a drowning."

"That just means you need to find his doctor." Cora tapped her fist softly on the table. "Time's a wastin'!"

"I'll try to give Paxton a push tomorrow for you. That's all I can do. What do you have planned for the weekend?"

"I'm headed to the community center in the morning. Peggy starts the quilt show at ten o'clock, so I asked Vicki to make some extra muffins for me. I'm going by the Fennel Street Bakery first to pick up breakfast for everyone. That way I can check on Arlene and the event at the same time."

"I heard Georgia talking about it at the station. She's planning to go down there."

"Peggy seems a little nervous about this one for some reason. Maybe because this is her first time demonstrating. I'll have to go back out there in the evening because Dorothy Parish has the Merchants Association meeting at seven o'clock."

"Well, Bert Miller is having a subdivision meeting tomorrow. It seems Miriam has stirred everyone up again and there may be a revolt out on Lavender Lane."

"Are you going out there?"

"No, I think it's just for the homeowners, but I told Bert to let me know what they decide to do. Miriam sent everyone a notice for a meeting on Monday evening and Bert's meeting is for everyone to get their ducks in a row first."

"What does Miriam want this time? Pfft, that woman needs a hobby!"

"I think she has one. Unfortunately, it seems her hobby is terrorizing everyone else."

Cora Mae giggled. "Sadly, it does."

"She's proposing that they form a homeowners association out there, and Bert says she promised not to do that when he bought the lot."

"How does she benefit if they have an HOA? She doesn't even live out there?" Cora shuddered. "Did she just need a new way to upset the whole neighborhood?"

"Well, my only guess is that she thinks she'll get the HOA dues and use them to make the subdivision look better. I think she's having trouble selling the last of the lots."

"Oh, that woman isn't hurting for money," Cora scoffed. "She's squeezed every drop she can from her renters. Those poor people live in fear of eviction every month. I'm sure Miriam Landry's bank account is doing fine."

"I don't know her motivation, but it's got Bert shook up enough to talk about moving."

"Joyce will not like hearing that."

"So, when you talked to Arlene, did she mention Larry Langley at all?" Conrad draped his napkin in his lap when he saw the waiter headed toward their table.

"I brought it up and all she said was that Larry didn't bother Hobart. He had felt positive about the meeting last night." Cora leaned back when the waiter delivered their dinners. "Thank you."

"I'm wondering if Arlene even knew about the signs disappearing. Saucy told me that he talked to Hobart about it, but Hobart may not have bothered her with it. I'll give her a little time and then I think I need to ask her a few questions."

"Are you going to talk with Larry?" Cora dunked her tea bag in her cup.

"No, not unless Detective Snell asks me to do that."

Cora Mae waved her hand dismissively and passed Conrad the salt.

"I'm surprised that the Sheriff's office is being as cordial as they are. I don't want to give them any reason to shut me out."

"I guess so, but I'd sure like to know how Larry is handling the news of Hobart's death. It was the only way he had any chance of winning this election." Cora Mae furrowed her forehead and glanced across the table at Conrad.

"Hmm, that sounds like motive to me."

"Yes, it does," Cora Mae said as she pointed her finger in the air. "I wonder how long it will take Detective Snell to realize that."

CHAPTER EIGHT

"Working the weekend, Chief?" Officer Fred Rucker waved when Conrad walked in the door to the Spicetown Police Department in uniform. He worked some Saturdays if he needed to catch up, but he usually dressed in street clothes to do that. This Saturday morning, he knew there were things that needed to be done, whether he was officially asked to do them or not.

"Morning, Fred. Yeah, I've got a little this and that to do. Everything okay last night?"

"Reports are on your desk. Nothing out of the ordinary."

"Good. Thanks, Fred." Conrad readied his coffee machine and quickly looked through the reports from the previous night while he waited for the water to heat.

When Conrad's phone began to ring, he pulled out his desk chair and grabbed it. "Chief Harris."

"Morning, Chief. This is Sam Snell in Paxton."

"Good morning, Detective. Have you heard anything?"

"I don't have the autopsy report. They said it would be at least Monday before that's ready, but Deputy Coroner York talked to the Sheriff. He said there are signs of a struggle so this can't automatically be ruled an accident. He recommended we develop the scene and do some preliminary interviews. I didn't know if you'd be available today, but I--"

"I am at your disposal."

"Great. Well, I haven't talked to the spouse at all, so I thought I'd start there today."

"The wife is not home today. She's down at the community center helping with a quilt show."

"Oh, you've talked to her?"

"Not today, but I know that she planned to go down there. She stayed overnight with a friend last night and that friend is the lady coordinating the quilt show, so I'm assuming that's where she's at now."

"Oh," Detective Snell stammered. "Well, I have to secure the scene, take some pictures and re-interview Hazel Linton. Maybe after that, Mrs. Emery will be available."

"I'd not be surprised if Hazel isn't at the quilt show, too. I could be wrong." Conrad chuckled. "Maybe we just need to go to the quilt show."

"Good grief. Well, if it's okay, I'll be over there in an hour and we'll see what we need to do."

"Sounds good. Thanks for calling." Conrad filled his travel mug with his chicory and sat down to make some notes. He hoped this would give him another chance to provide some input into the investigation. He made a short list of names and planned to encourage the detective to look outside of Hobart's home for a possible killer.

§

"Morning, Mayor." Vicki Garvin waved from behind the counter at the Fennel Street Bakery when Cora Mae came in Saturday morning. Cora waved back but had to stop at a table to chat before making it up to the counter.

"Good morning, Vicki! Are you coming down to the community center when the morning rush is over?"

"I sure am. I told Peggy I'd man the tables so she could go to lunch if she wanted to get out of there for a few minutes. I know it's tough when you feel like you can't leave."

"That's really nice of you. I think she has Arlene sitting with her."

"How is Arlene doing? I saw the paper this morning. I'm so shocked about Hobart." Vicki closed the pastry case and grabbed two white boxes for Cora.

"She stayed with Peggy last night and I think it's good for her not to be alone right away."

"Give her my love, will you?" Vicki handed the white boxes over the high counter to Cora Mae.

"I will, Vicki. Thank you. I'll see you tonight at the Merchants Association meeting."

"Is that tonight? Oh, I'm glad you mentioned it. I'd forgotten. Yes, I'll be there."

Cora waved and pushed through the front doors to walk the short way to the community center. It was a beautiful sunny day with that special cooling snap in the air that only autumn provides. She wanted to cherish it as long as possible. If the weather was always this kind, she would turn in her car and walk everywhere, but she knew these days were fleeting. As Cora walked through the lobby of the community center and pulled open the auditorium doors, she had to pause a moment to adjust to the absence of the theater seating. The transformation always shocked her. Even the lighting was different.

Long banquet tables lined one side of the room where vendors were setting up their wares to display or sell and the other side had quilts draped from high hanging clips. All heads were bowed over their work when Cora Mae sneaked up behind them.

"Have you worked up an appetite yet?" Cora held up the white pastry boxes. "This is me bringing my talent to the table!"

Peggy laughed and extended her arms to take the boxes. "Oh, thank you, Cora. I'm so hungry. I rushed this morning to make sure I could get everything here on time and didn't get a bite to eat."

"Problem solved!" Cora smiled as Arlene approached. "Well, hello there. Is Peggy working you too hard? I brought some muffins."

"Oh, no. I'm enjoying the excitement. Have you seen all the beautiful quilts? I'm so happy I could help her out. I was going to run to the bakery and get us something to eat once things calmed down. We have coffee. Would you like some?" Arlene pointed to a large coffee urn set up on a table against the wall.

"No, thank you. I do want to see the quilts though. I had hoped to get over there before everyone else does, but I see the doors are open." Cora pointed to the people walking into the auditorium.

"Oh, goodness." Arlene threw her hands in the air. "I better get back to my station."

Cora Mae strolled to the other side of the auditorium and studied the signs posted next to each design with the quilter's name and pattern information. Maybe she would give this a try when she retired. Her seamstress talents were limited to basic repair and hemming slacks, but she understood the basic function. Several of the quilts were variations of the Ohio Star pattern and she would love to have one of her own. When she came across a nine-patch lap quilt and saw Arlene's name as the artist, she glanced over to the demonstration tables to see if she could catch Arlene's eye. What she saw instead had her skittering across the auditorium as inconspicuously as possible.

Miriam Landry was standing at Arlene's table talking to her and although Cora couldn't see Miriam's face, she could see shock and bewilderment registering across Arlene's face.

"Miriam! Surprising to see you here today," Cora said with every intention of interrupting whatever Miriam was doing to Arlene.

Miriam's head whipped around. "Cora." Her greetings were delivered on a dismissive sneer. Cora and Miriam had a history.

"Please let me know," Miriam said to Arlene and then handed her a business card before walking toward the door.

Arlene didn't comment, but her face was pale. Cora ran around the banquet table to take the chair beside Arlene. "Are you okay? What did she say?"

"Oh, Cora. I don't know what to do. Miriam wants to know what I plan to do with the lot Hobart purchased in her subdivision. I don't know. He had plans, but I don't know if it's-- I can't think about that now."

"Of course you can't, and you don't have to tell her anything. It's none of her business. If Hobart bought it, it's no longer her concern. Forget you ever saw her." Cora squeezed Arlene's arm.

"But she offered to buy it back. Strange, isn't it? I mean, why would she do that? She can't be doing it to help me out."

"Maybe she got an offer for it at a higher price." Cora shrugged. "That sounds more like Miriam."

"It does. Maybe that's it. I'm not doing anything with it right now. That's the least of my problems. You're right. I'm going to forget this even happened."

"That's the best idea. I came over here to tell you I saw your lap quilt. It's lovely. I had no idea you had an entry today. Are you selling it?"

"No, I just brought it for display. I made it for Hobart's sister. I used the fabrics from her home, and I hoped it would help with her memory."

"Does she know about Hobart?" Cora wondered if Arlene would continue to care for her sister-in-law as Hobart had done.

"No. I tried but I couldn't connect with her last night on the phone. She has good days, but I'm not sure telling her is even the right thing to do."

"She might just be happier thinking he will come visit her soon." Cora looked up when a customer approached Arlene with a question about the pattern books for sale on the table.

Slipping away from the table, Cora waved when she saw Conrad walk through the doors.

"Do you have a minute?" Conrad looked from one side of the room to the other. "Can you step out in the lobby with me?"

Cora followed quickly behind Conrad as he walked to the far side of the lobby away from the doors.

"You have news?" Cora was anxious for the coroner's report.

"How do you think in there? It's like listening to a radio station that isn't quite tuned in to the station. I have a headache already."

Cora Mae chuckled as she shook her head.

"I saw you talking to Arlene. Is she doing all right today?"

"She was until Miriam Landry came in and rattled her. Did you know that Hobart bought one of Miriam's subdivision lots?"

Conrad shook his head and frowned. "They were going to build out there? Well, I guess it would have put him right next to his farmland, but I wouldn't have ever guessed Hobart would move. They've got a great property now."

"I got the impression from Arlene that Hobart had other plans for the land. She didn't indicate they were going to build a house out there." Cora waved at some ladies entering the lobby and turned back to Conrad. "Miriam came in here a few minutes ago and asked Arlene what she planned to do with the lot and offered to buy it back from her."

"She's gotten a higher offer." Conrad nodded and jutted his chin forward. "She's wheeling and dealing as usual."

"That's what I thought, but why wouldn't that person just make the offer to Arlene? Buy it from Arlene instead? Is it so much more that Miriam wants to flip it?"

"They must not have known about Hobart's purchase and Miriam is trying to finagle it, so she gets to make the more profitable deal."

Cora shook her head in disappointment and then remembered it was Conrad who had something to share. "What was your news?"

"Got a call from the county this morning. Detective Snell wants to investigate now." Conrad smiled.

"And what changed his mind?"

"He said Deputy Coroner York doesn't have an autopsy report yet, but he sees signs of struggle. Based on that, the Sheriff said he should work it like it's real." Conrad chuckled at the opportunity to use his own catch phrase. He always told his staff not to worry about deciding whether something was a crime or not. When they get a report, they should work it like it's a real crime until they find out because you can't go back and fix things you miss.

"So, you are interviewing today." That explained the uniform and the early morning visit. Saturdays were usually more casual and involved play time with Briscoe, Conrad's police canine and pet.

"Yeah, Snell is on his way over. He wanted to talk to Arlene, and he said he needed to secure the scene. I'd like to go out to his farm and also try talking to Hazel again."

"You aren't taking Briscoe? He might help if you have to interview Larry. He's terribly afraid of Briscoe." Cora Mae laughed.

"I didn't know that."

"He complained about him in one of our council meetings one day. He claimed Briscoe gave him the evil eye on the street one day and he felt that police canines opened the city up to possible litigation for threatening and harassing witnesses during interrogations." Cora held her arms out at her sides and imitated Larry on his soap box. "He felt intimidated by Briscoe's expression."

"Good to know," Conrad smiled. "Briscoe is busy today. He went hiking with Gwen out on the lake trails. She was trying to get Tabor to go with her, but I'm not sure if she talked him into it or not. She came by early this morning and picked Briscoe up and I forgot to ask her, but he'll be busy all day. She's taken quite a fancy to Briscoe and the feeling seems to be mutual."

"Well, they have a lovely day for their hike. I walked here myself today."

"From your house?" Conrad's eyes widened.

"No, silly. From the bakery. I thought it would offset the cinnamon roll I was planning to eat."

Conrad hooked his thumbs in his belt as his laughter shook his belly. "A whole block! I may have to try that."

"You should. I highly recommend it," Cora Mae said pointing a finger at his chest before turning to walk back into the auditorium. "Talk to you later."

CHAPTER NINE

"Morning, Chief! Glad you're free today." Sam Snell rocked on his toes in Conrad's doorway and looked up and down the hallway.

"Coffee?"

"No, I've had plenty. Have you had a chance to reach out to Mrs. Emery?"

"Have a seat." Conrad motioned to Detective Snell to take a chair in his office. His antics in the doorway were making Conrad nervous. "I found Mrs. Emery down at the quilt show this morning, but Mrs. Linton is home, if we want to visit her again."

"Great." Detective Snell pulled his phone from his pocket and glanced at it. "Sorry. I've got a heavy caseload right now and there's a lot going on."

"I understand."

"That's why I appreciate your help here."

"I'm happy to help any way that I can." Conrad tapped his pen on his notepad. "Do you want to start with the lake this morning?"

"Yeah. I wish I'd let the techs collect everything yesterday, but I really didn't think this was going to blow up on me. I thought it was just a bad accident. They got pictures where the body was found, but that's all that was collected."

Conrad nodded. "I always tell my guys to work it like it's real, then you don't have any regrets later."

Detective Snell nodded. "Hmm, good advice. Is Officer Kimball around today? Is she going to join us?"

"No, we might see her out there. She's off today, but she said she was going to walk the lake trails. She's new to this area and she's trying out some things."

"Oh, really? I didn't realize she wasn't from the area."

"She's from Minnesota. She worked for her local police department up there, and we hired her this summer. She's still exploring."

"Wow! Very interesting. She seemed very capable."

Conrad nodded.

"I'm ready to get to it. We can start at the lake first." Detective Snell popped up from his seat. " I'll follow you out there."

Conrad grabbed his jacket, and when the detective left through the side door, Conrad walked down to the dispatch cubicle and told Officer Fred Rucker where he was going before leaving through the front door.

Conrad pulled his squad car up behind Hobart Emery's truck and stopped. He would need to tell Arlene to get this towed unless Detective Snell wanted to have it fingerprinted. As the detective unloaded his camera and crime scene supplies from his trunk, Conrad inspected the bed of Hobart's truck. It looked immaculate. No grass, dirt, or any fishing gear. That seemed unusual for a farmer.

"Is it unlocked?" Detective Snell walked around the truck.

Conrad pulled a glove on his right hand and lifted the handle. "No, it's locked."

Snell peered in the window and shrugged before walking down the slope toward the docks. "You want to look around while I take some pictures?"

"Sure," Conrad said. "I'll take a look at the boat. He should have his fishing gear in there somewhere. Was his phone in his personal affects?"

"Yeah," Detective Snell said. "Clothes, wallet and phone."

“What did Deputy York say about his exam?"

"Well, he had contusions on his face, the left side of his head, and some bruising on the top. He also had bruising and cuts on his fingers with some wood particles under his nails."

"That may be from the dock." Conrad pointed. "Or it could be from this oar."

"Was that here yesterday?" Snell frowned.

"The oar? Yeah, it was here, but if he fell here and drifted down to the Linton's, he could have hit any of these docks." Conrad nodded and stepped into Hobart's boat. Squatting down, he looked at the tackle box and poles sitting to one side. "His stuff is in here, so we know he made it this far. I'm surprised he didn't remove the signs from the boat."

"Like I said before, they may not have been a surprise. He may have put them there and planned to take them out to dump in the lake." Snell chuckled.

Conrad frowned. "He had to do something with them because they're in the way." Conrad stepped around them and looked at the tackle box. It seemed silly to think Hobart was just going to ignore them in the middle of his boat. "Do you want the signs sent to the lab?"

"Do you think that's necessary?" Sam scowled.

Conrad didn't answer. It wasn't his call, but if it had been, it would all get pulled and tagged.

"What's across there?" Detective Snell pointed across the lake. "Anybody live over there? Maybe they saw something."

"Nobody lives there. It's an old fishing camp that hasn't been in use since before I moved to

Spicetown. Doesn't mean there aren't squatters over there. Maybe you could ask your office to check and see if there have been any reports filed on activity in that area."

"Good idea."

Conrad hummed. He was hearing that a lot, but he wasn't expecting much follow-up. "His tackle box and poles are here."

"So, he got in the boat?"

"Not necessarily." Conrad stepped back up on the dock. "He could have placed them in the boat while standing on the dock. I'd like to print the yard signs if you don't care. I'd like to know if he put them here or not."

"Oh, yeah." Detective Snell handed the fingerprint kit to Conrad. "That might help with your case."

Conrad smirked as he stepped back in the boat. It wasn't worth explaining again. If Hobart handled just the top sign, it might mean he had discovered them in his boat. If his prints were on the bottom sign, it would indicate he put them there. It was an odd storage location choice for a man who owned a truck, had a two-car garage, and several barns on a farm. Why would he put Larry Langley's yard signs in his boat?

"So how was this election thing going? I mean, you said it was high-profile. Was this guy expected to win?"

"Hmm, it was leaning his way. The opponent, Larry Langley, is the incumbent. Hobart was new on the political scene, but Larry has had some image problems of late."

"So, that's why you suggested I talk to the Langley guy? He has a motive to take Emery out?" Detective Snell peered into the boat at the yard signs.

Conrad wasn't pointing fingers. "It would be appropriate to include him on your list of suspects. Yes."

"I've taken pictures of the boat interior. You can set the signs up on the dock. I guess I'll take them in with me."

Conrad began tagging each yard sign in the order it was stacked in the boat until the bottom sign was exposed. Dusting each side of the sign with powder, he placed tape over the impressions to lift the prints with the tape and place them on an evidence card.

"I'll wrap up the signs now, if you're done with them." Detective Snell began going through his evidence bag.

"Yeah, I'm done." Conrad strolled around the dock. "Any scratches on the edges?"

"Huh?" Detective Snell looked over his shoulder.

"Did you see any signs of scratches around the sides of the dock? Didn't you say the coroner found wood slivers under his nails?" Conrad's eyebrows furrowed.

"Oh, yeah. No, I didn't. Take a look, would ya?" Detective Snell struggled with the tape to seal his evidence and muttered under his breath.

"You've got scratches down here on the end. They look fresh to me." Conrad picked up the detective's camera and crouched down on the edge of the dock to take photos. There could be hair and fibers embedded in these rough wood edges, but Detective Snell didn't seem to show any interest.

"I'll bag the oar for you. I'd recommend you send it to the lab for prints instead of us trying to pull them here. The wood is pretty worn."

"Yeah, okay. Did you find the other oar in the boat?"

"Other oar?"

"Well, shouldn't there be two oars?" Detective Snell flung out his hand in question.

Conrad kept his face expressionless. "No, generally in this type of boat, you would only have one."

Snell frowned and then shrugged both shoulders. "I'm going to load this stuff in my car. I think I'll leave Mrs. Linton to you and I'll go see if the spouse is at home yet."

"Okay. Sounds good." Conrad nodded.

§

"Hello, Paulie!" Cora patted Paulie Childers on the back. "I'm glad to see you are hard at work today. There's a lot going on in Spicetown. Are you here to do a story on the quilt show or were you planning to stay around and cover the Spicetown Merchants Association meeting?"

"Hi mayor. I'm doing a piece on the quilt show, but I'm glad I ran into you. I've been trying to reach the police chief and I can't catch him. Have you seen him?"

Cora Mae chuckled. "He was here earlier this morning, but he's out of town all day. You know, I'm glad I ran into you."

"You are?" Paulie frowned.

"I am." Cora patted his back as they turned to walk through the quilt demonstration. "You know there is an issue that really needs some attention, and the Spicetown Star is the perfect place."

"What issue is that?"

"There are going to be a lot of questions that the citizens will have in response to candidate Emery's death. I'm sure his name will be on the ballot because it's too late to change that. I would like to encourage you to contact the city attorney for guidance."

"Ned?"

"Yes, Ned Carey will know what has to be done next and everyone needs to know that before the election. Do you think you could share that concern with your editor?"

"Hmm, I guess so."

"I really think the newspaper is the best way to get this information out to the voters. The

Spicetown Star has been so involved this year in helping keep citizens apprised of election news. This would be an important topic to cover right now."

"I see your point. I'll see what I can do."

"Thank you, Paulie." Cora smiled as she walked away.

CHAPTER TEN

"Hazel, there's no need to apologize. It should have shaken you up. I hope finding a dead body never becomes an ordinary occurrence around here."

"I should hope not." Hazel's husband, Paul, handed Hazel a cup of tea and sat down in the chair next to her.

"Thank you, dear. You know, Chief, I almost went outside yesterday when I saw Hobart. I wanted to tell him how sorry I was that Larry Langley had acted the way he did Thursday night. It was shameful."

"Larry has some anger problems," Paul said. "He always has had, but I think they're getting worse with age."

"He was out here earlier Friday and I almost went outside and gave him a piece of my mind." Hazel gave a curt nod. "I have to admit I'm a little frightened of him right now, after seeing how he's behaved, and with Paul not here, I decided I better keep my opinion to myself."

"Aw, I don't think he would ever hurt you. He might say something off color, though." Paul chuckled.

"Hazel, Larry was out here Friday morning?"

"Yes, early, before Hobart arrived."

"Does he have his boat out here?"

"No, not anymore. He was here to pull it out. I watched him hook it up. He does it every year. He doesn't store it out here in the winter."

"Why not?" Conrad made a note in his pad. Snell needed to have this information tonight.

"He's got cover for it at his place," Paul said. "He's got a big pole barn at home. He just doesn't want to drag it back and forth all summer. His kids use it a lot. He puts it in the water in the spring and pulls it out to store in the fall."

"What dock was his?" Conrad flipped his notebook back open, but he knew the answer already.

"Oh, it's right next to Hobart's." Hazel chuckled. "I don't know if they're even aware of it because they're never here at the same time."

"Hazel, did you see Larry leave? You said you watched him pull his boat out. Did you actually see him drive down Eagle Bay Road?"

"No. I was baking an apple strudel and I guess he drove off when I was in the kitchen. I just saw him pull his boat up the ramp, but it was probably thirty minutes or so before I saw Hobart arrive."

"So, you saw Hobart drive up and park?"

"Well, no," Hazel stammered. "I saw Hobart down on the dock."

"Was he in his boat?"

"No, he was on the dock and then I went to put some laundry in the dryer before we sat down to eat."

"Hazel, let me make sure I have this timeline correct. You saw Larry pulling his boat out of the water and you saw Hobart half an hour later on his own dock, but you didn't see him arrive. Is that correct?"

"Yes. It's not like I sit and look out the window all day, Conrad. I just glance out there every so often if there's activity."

"I understand, Hazel. It's just that I want to make sure I've got it right before I give it to the Sheriff's office. This is their case and I'm just helping them out with some leg work." Conrad stood up. "Thank you both for your time."

Paul stood and reached his hand out to shake, following Conrad to the front door. "It's possible Larry was still here when Hobart got here. Hazel doesn't want that to be true, but it's possible."

Conrad nodded. "Thank you, Paul."

§

"Can I have everyone's attention?" Bert Miller held his arms up in the air and addressed the crowd huddled around on his back deck and backyard. "I don't want anyone to feel pressured.

We are going to do this by secret ballot. We just need to know where we stand. If we aren't all together, that's okay. We just need to be prepared before Monday." Bert Miller passed out ballots to all of his neighbors. The weather had been lovely, and Joyce had put together tables outside for everyone to eat together. With the meal behind them, it was time to talk business.

"Bert, have you talked to Miriam?" Earl Lester lived next door to Bert, and they had discussed calling Miriam.

"No. I was afraid to call her. I was so angry when I got that letter, and I didn't want to make the situation more adversarial."

Earl nodded his approval. He had recommended Bert not take that step.

"And my wife told me not to," Bert said, pointing at Joyce. Everyone laughed and it eased the tension while they filled out the handmade ballots Joyce had put together.

"Did you invite Mrs. Emery?" Felicia Ward asked the question of Joyce, but Bert heard her and looked around the crowd.

"Did everybody know that Hobart Emery bought a lot out here? Everybody but me?" There were murmurs around the group.

"I only know because I was in the Carom Seed Craft Corner when Mrs. Emery was in there talking to the owner about it." Felicia dropped her ballot in the flower vase Joyce was using to collect the results.

"I wonder what she'll decide to do with the lot now." Earl Lester said what everyone else thought.

"While we're waiting on the tally, help yourself to some dessert. We have cakes and ice cream. Dig in!" Bert followed Joyce into the house to count.

§

Conrad parked his car near the barn door and looked around the farm. Seeing someone at a nearby storage shed, he climbed out of his car.

"Evening," Conrad said with a tip of his hat. "Sorry to keep you, but I'm looking for Ted Aldridge."

"I'm Ted. Evening, Chief. How can I help you?" Ted locked up the storage shed and pocketed the keys.

"Just a few routine questions. Mrs. Emery said Hobart was out here Friday morning. Did you see him?"

"Yeah, we went over a few things. He came out pretty regular and checked on stuff. He wasn't here long." Ted began walking toward the barn, so Conrad followed.

"Did Hobart seem his usual self on Friday morning?" Conrad scratched his head. "Did you notice anything out of the ordinary in how he looked or what he said?"

"Nope. Grouchy as usual. That was just Hobart's way."

"Did he talk about the town hall meeting he had the night before?"

"No, but we don't talk about personal stuff. He's my boss. That's all."

"It doesn't sound like you thought much of Hobart. Did you two get along okay?"

Ted stopped and put his hands at his waist. "He don't pay me to like him. He pays me to take care of the farm business and I do that."

"You two argue?"

"About every other day," Ted chuckled. "Hobart was a hardheaded horse's behind most of the time. Smart man, though. Knew what he was doing. He just didn't tolerate any tomfoolery and didn't think twice about firing somebody if they made a mistake."

"So, there are some ex-employees out there that might hold a grudge?" Conrad raised his eyebrows in question.

"Might be."

"Would you be willing to make a list of those past and present employees for Detective Snell? This is a Sheriff's Department case and I'm just helping them out. I'm sure they'd like to have that information."

"I guess I can do that."

"Good. Thank you. Can you drop it off at the police department tomorrow? I'll send it over to Paxton for you."

"Will do." Ted saluted and turned back to unlock his truck. He was a man of few words, so few Conrad wasn't sure if he just might be one of the disgruntled employees.

CHAPTER ELEVEN

Cora Mae had hoped to say a few words at the opening of the Spicetown Merchants Association meeting and skedaddle out of there, however Dorothy had not supported that plan. Dorothy Parish wanted Cora to wrap the meeting up for her with words of encouragement and support. Cora sat off to the side in a folding chair with her mind miles away as Dorothy and Frank outlined their vision of the Merchants Association. Cora could picture Arlene Emery sitting in an empty house, and that image plunged her into the despair of her own memories.

When Cora realized that Dorothy had been going around the room to solicit input from the participants, she snapped to and swiveled in her chair.

"Hi, everyone. My name is Kelly Vaughn and I currently live in Paxton, but my husband and I are moving to Spicetown soon. We are hoping to open a business here, and that's why I attended your meeting tonight. My husband, Aaron, is working, so I'm here to gather information and meet everyone." Kelly scrunched up her shoulders and smiled. She was a young girl, early twenties, and her smile was familiar, but Cora didn't know the name Vaughn.

"What made you pick Spicetown?" Dorothy held up her hands. "I know it's a wonderful place to live, but what drew you to our little town?"

"Oh, I'm from Spicetown. This is where I grew up."

"Ah, so you already know it's a wonderful place." Frank Parish chuckled. "We're glad you're coming home. Was there some information in particular that you were hoping to find out tonight or something that the Merchants Association might be able to help you with?"

"Our biggest obstacle right now is whether we can get a business license in Spicetown. My husband has talked to the City Council, but we haven't applied yet. He says they weren't too receptive when he met with them, and he hoped the Merchants Association was in a position to help new businesses get established."

"Well, that's a new item for our list!" Dorothy wrote down a note on her pad. "That's an idea that hasn't been presented, but we will certainly consider what kind of service we could provide. This is a newly formed group, and we are just developing our mission. Anyone else have a service idea to add to the list?" A hand went up in the back and Dorothy pointed to Jeff Wiggins.

"Evening, everyone. I'm Jeff Wiggins and I own the Spicetown Rock Quarry. One of the things I find that I've needed over the years is legal help. Not enough to keep an attorney on retainer, but occasionally I've needed some legal advice and I didn't know where to turn. I'm hoping since there's a group of us together, maybe we could have some kind of legal adviser that's available to us."

"Do you mean like for filing corporation paperwork?" Frank Parish asked.

"That, too. My situation was a partnership agreement. I wish I'd had some legal help with that in the past. It also comes into play when you sell a part of the business. Those kinds of things are something that you need a legal eye to look over. I feel like I was taken advantage of because I didn't have that kind of help at the time. It's just one of those things you wish you would have done differently, and new businesses probably run across a lot of times when they could use some legal advice."

"Oh, I agree," Dorothy said. "I'll definitely add that item. It would be nice to have a legal counsel we could keep on retainer for simple questions and guidance. If you needed them for something big, they could quote you a price with maybe a little merchants association member discount, but just an ear for the simple stuff would be a great idea. Thank you, Jeff."

"Anyone else? Did we miss anything?" Frank held up his hands.

"We have gathered some great information tonight and we will send out some minutes for the meeting to each of you by email. If you're interested in joining a committee to do some research and development on these items, please indicate that on the sheet that's being passed around." Dorothy looked at Cora Mae and nodded. "Mayor Bingham, would you like to say a few words?"

"Hello, everyone." Cora walked to the front of the group. "I just wanted to tell you that City Hall is delighted with the development of this association and so eager for all of you to become active participants in a coalition that will support Spicetown commerce. We all struggle to handle things alone in life, but when you are fortunate enough to live in a community such as we do, you quickly learn that you are never alone. I want to welcome our potential new business," Cora said as she pointed at Kelly Vaughn. "I hope the Merchants Association becomes just another reason why entrepreneurs seek out Spicetown for a business location. This town is growing every day and with that growth means we need to provide for those citizens. I'm sure Dorothy and Frank will keep me updated on your progress, but just know that the City Council and I support your goals."

"Goodnight, everyone. You'll hear from me soon." Dorothy spoke over the light applause and Cora Mae waved to the group as they began disbursing.

"I think it went well," Frank said to Cora as she slipped on her coat. "There seems to be a strong interest. Now we just need to see if we can really pull together something worthwhile for everyone."

"Do you think Ned Carey would agree to be available to members if we paid him a retainer fee?" Dorothy glanced at her notebook. "I had thought about legal advice. I wasn't sure if anyone else would be interested, but I know there have been times when I could have used it, too."

"I really don't know what kind of workload Ned is dealing with right now," Cora said. "I think he would if he had the time."

"Did you know about the new business the young girl mentioned?" Dorothy tilted her head towards the door where Kelly was walking out.

"A young man from Paxton did talk to the City Council about a franchise. He hasn't applied for a business license yet, but he did make a proposal. You know the council has always been very divided on that issue. I don't know which way they would go."

"You mean that girl is the Burger Buddy? The question from the town hall meeting. Was that about her?" Dorothy tapped her notepad. "I wondered where that came from."

"It may be. I know it's an issue that Hobart and Larry didn't agree on, and there are other members on the council that are split on the issue."

"What do you think?" Frank asked. "Do you think Spicetown should have franchised fast-food?"

"It's never been an issue I've had to vote on," Cora smiled. "See you both later. I need to get home and feed Marmalade. She'll think something has happened to me." With her hands fluttering in the air, Cora bustled from the auditorium, relieved that she was finally headed home and pleased at how she avoided answering that question.

§

When Conrad returned to the Police Department, Briscoe had been lounging under the dispatch desk. He had seemed pleased to see Conrad, but not interested enough to get up. When he realized Conrad was going to work for a while in his office, he had moved to the big sheepskin dog bed under the window in the Chief's office and stretched out.

Typing up his notes, he wondered if Detective Snell had been paying attention when he had first explained the dynamics of the relationship between Hobart and Larry Langley. If he had, he might jump to conclusions based on what Hazel was reporting. Hazel had not seen the two meet. She had merely seen them both there that morning.

Ted Aldridge had surprised Conrad in his attitude. Most people over compensated when they talked to the police and when they talked about someone that had recently died. They had a tendency to underplay any hostility or negativity toward that person. Ted had seemed very straightforward in his mere tolerance of Hobart. He appeared to have a quiet respect for Hobart's knowledge, but clearly did not have any warm feelings toward his employer.

As Conrad sent his email to Detective Snell with his reports attached, he glanced at the clock. His stomach had already told him it was dinner time for both of them.

"Let's go home, Briscoe. We're going to get dinner and relax. Tomorrow is a day off. I've got big plans to do nothing all day. Are you game?"

Conrad slipped his coat on and Briscoe stood ready at the door. After the election next week, things should calm down.

CHAPTER TWELVE

Arlene wiped down the kitchen counter again and decided to water her plants. Everyone seemed to think she should be at home, but she had no direction here. Her house was clean, she had no appetite, and it was raining outside, so she couldn't do yard work. She didn't want to think about her situation. She needed a distraction. A knock on her screen door that Sunday afternoon was a welcome sound.

Miriam Landry stood on Arlene's porch with wide eyes and glared over at the large black Labrador Retriever sitting beside her on the porch happily thumping his tail against the floor.

"Hello, Miriam!" Arlene opened the screen door. "Come in."

"Thank you. I'm sorry to intrude and I apologize if I upset you yesterday."

"Can I get you some coffee or tea?" Arlene draped Miriam's coat over a kitchen chair.

"No. No, I won't keep you. I just wanted to explain myself. I know I've been accused of being insensitive but that was not my intention. Hobart and I had our disagreements, and I'm sorry about my timing, but I do need to have some idea of your intentions. You see--"

"Miriam, I don't know what my future plans are. I would happily share that information with you if I had everything figured out, but I just don't. There's a lot to think about and I can't make any decisions right now."

"Tomorrow evening I have a meeting planned for the homeowners out on Lavender Lane. I invited Hobart and I wanted to make sure you were aware of the meeting in case you would like to attend. The meeting is being held to discuss forming a homeowners association and as a property owner, you would have a vote in that decision."

"I don't think I'm interested in attending. I think the people living out there now should make that decision and I'll abide by their choice."

"Okay, I will tell them that and I won't keep you. I am sorry for your loss."

"Thank you, Miriam. I appreciate it." Arlene handed Miriam her coat without any threat of tears. Somehow the sentiment didn't ring true.

§

Cora Mae reached over to turn off the burner under her gravy when she heard the doorbell ring. She had invited Conrad over for Sunday night dinner and it was almost ready. After church she had taken the afternoon to relax and recharge.

"Come on in. My biscuits aren't out yet, but everything else is ready." Cora hung Conrad's jacket on the coat tree and hurried back to the kitchen.

"Smells good."

"I'll have to warn you, my healthy kick has passed." Cora chuckled. She had been trying to watch what she ate and focus on healthy foods, but that had gotten boring. She had been craving fried chicken all day and that's what she made.

"I never was on a health kick. That was your thing, so I don't mind a bit." Conrad opened the cabinet and began to set the table. He had eaten Sunday dinner at Cora Mae's house many times and knew exactly where the plates and glasses were kept.

"Any news today or did you get to take a break?" Cora poured the gravy into a bowl and carried it to the table.

"I got a copy of Detective Snell's report on his conversation with Arlene. Do you want sweet tea to drink?"

"Yes, please." The timer dinged and Cora pulled open the oven door to remove her biscuits.

"I remember you telling me about Larry Langley making an allegation that Hobart was still involved in the rock quarry." Conrad placed the silverware on the table and pulled out a chair.

"Yes, he said Hobart drew a pension or was being paid in some manner by the quarry. I told him that it was not the same as being employed or involved in the function of the business."

"Snell asked Arlene about Hobart's pension and she said the rock quarry owed Hobart money and he was taking it in installments. He didn't have a traditional pension."

Cora carried the last serving dish to the table and pulled out her chair. "I hope she has something in place to ensure she continues to receive those payments."

"It didn't read that way, but Snell didn't really ask those questions. Arlene told him she had a life insurance policy on Hobart and that she was the beneficiary. I think that was what he was more concerned about."

"I don't think she knows what she has. I asked her a couple of questions about that yesterday and she just told me that Rick Manning said she was taken care of, that Hobart had make arrangements for her. Rick sells insurance but he's no financial adviser. She seems to trust him, but I think she's operating on blind faith."

"Maybe she can keep running the farm. I'm hoping to get Detective Snell back out to the farm so he can try talking to Ted Aldridge. I didn't get much from him. Is he from Spicetown?"

"She says she gets along well with Ted, but that he and Hobart argued a lot." Cora grabbed another napkin. "I'm not sure where Ted lives now, but he didn't grow up here."

"He's a pretty tight-lipped guy. I need to find out more about him. I'm hoping Arlene can fill me in. The chicken is good."

"Thank you. I just had a taste for it today."

"Where's Marmalade?" Conrad looked under the table and under his chair. Cora's orange tabby cat always greeted him, and he had just realized she hadn't appeared since he arrived.

Cora glanced under the table and around the room. "I don't know. I wonder..." Cora got up and walked down the hallway. "Here she is."

Marmalade strolled into the kitchen with her head held high while testing her loudest indignant meow.

"Where was she?" Conrad looked down as she rubbed her face against his shin.

"She got locked in the bedroom. She sneaks in sometimes when I'm busy doing something and I don't realize she's in there. When I leave and shut the door, she gets trapped."

Conrad shook his head and looked down at Marmalade again just as his cell phone rang. "Sorry." Conrad pulled his phone out of his pocket. "It's Detective Snell."

Cora encouraged him to answer the phone, flapping her hands impatiently.

"Chief Harris... I did. Did you interview him today?"

Cora reached for the tea pitcher and refilled their glasses.

"You know the election is Tuesday, right?" Conrad rolled his eyes and shook his head at Cora.

"Okay, I'll see you at nine o'clock tomorrow morning. Thanks."

"What? What?" Cora fluttered her fingers in anticipation.

"You'll never believe this." Conrad huffed. "He's arrested Larry Langley."

"For what? Did I miss something?"

"Larry was out at the lake Friday morning. Snell went over to Larry's house this afternoon to get his statement, and Larry, true to form, acted like an idiot and got himself arrested."

"But the election is a day away!"

"I know, but they aren't charging him. At least not so far. He's just being held for questioning as a person of interest."

"Maybe he won't be there long." Despite their differences over the years, Cora was disappointed to see Larry lose his career over his inability to manage his self-destructive behavior.

"You know," Conrad said. "This news will leak tomorrow and everybody in town will know about this before they cast their ballot."

Cora Mae nodded her head. "If he had any chance of winning this election against a dead man, he just lost it."

CHAPTER THIRTEEN

"Good morning, Miss Morgan." Harvey Salzman bowed his head sheepishly in Amanda's doorway. "I know it's early, but I didn't see the mayor's car around back. Is she coming into the office today?"

"Hi, Mr. Salzman. Yes, as far as I know, she will be here. Is there something I can help you with?"

Saucy looked left and right before stepping over the threshold. Leaning forward and hunching his shoulders he whispered, "Did you hear that Larry Langley was arrested?"

Amanda smiled. "I did. My father told me it was in the paper this morning."

"Can you believe that? I was shocked. Do you think Larry could have killed Hobart Emery?"

"Oh, I don't know, Mr. Salzman. I couldn't say, but I don't think they've charged him with that. It may be nothing."

"That would explain the yard signs. Larry might have just gone off the deep end. You know, he's been acting like he's plum crazy lately. I don't know what to make of it!"

"Morning, Saucy," Cora Mae said as she walked through Amanda's door and into her office. "I bet I know what's gotten you out of the house so early today."

"Good morning, Mayor. I was just telling Miss Morgan that I was shocked, but Larry has been acting out lately. I couldn't believe what he said at the town hall meeting either. I was standing next to Luther Hoyle and I turned to him and said, 'Luther, what in tarnation is wrong with that boy!' Luther just shook his head. I can't make heads or tails out of what's been going on around here. Can you figure it out? Because I sure can't."

"I wish I had the answer to all that," Cora chuckled as she hung her coat behind the door. "I agree. He has been acting a bit out of sorts lately. Too much stress maybe."

"If that's the problem, he needs a vacation. He doesn't need to be running for City Council!"

"All that aside," Cora said, as she pulled open her desk drawer to park her handbag. "We have an election tomorrow."

"We do and I don't know how people are going to vote with neither candidate available. This is quite the conundrum."

"There is a third option." Cora sat down at her desk and pushed the button to start her computer. "There is always an option to vote for someone not on the ballot. You can write anyone's name in on your ballot."

Saucy gasped. "I hadn't even thought about that. You're right! Is that what you're going to do? That's brilliant. I need to give this some thought. I only have twenty-four hours and I need to think about who would be a good council member. There's really a lot to choose from when you think about it!"

"That's right. Don't worry about all this other stuff. You don't have much time. You have a serious decision to make!" Cora punched the air. "When you think of the best write-in candidate you need to let other people know. They probably haven't even thought of it either. To have an effective write-in campaign, you need supporters. Spread the word!"

Saucy spun around on his heels. "I'm on it, Mayor."

Amanda giggled as Saucy marched out her office door. "Did you give him marching orders?"

Cora chuckled. "I gave him something else to think about. With no viable council candidate, a serious write-in campaign could win this election. I don't know if he can master that in twenty-four hours, but I planted the seed."

"It's a good idea. Personally," Amanda said after looking over her shoulder. "I'm thinking about writing in Jimmy Kole's name. I've told him several times that he should try and run for the City Council."

Cora Mae nodded. "I would love to see that happen. I'd hate to lose him as my supervisor of

Streets & Alleys, but I think he's meant for greater things. I've told him that, but I don't know how he feels about it."

"If the citizens wrote him in, it might give him the confidence he needs to try it."

"It might. I don't know how people will react to Hobart's name on the ballot, but I don't think he'll get many votes considering the circumstances. If Larry is released today, he could win tomorrow. It's too late to reprint the ballots."

§

Conrad strolled down Fennel Street Monday morning just as the stores were opening. As he neared the Fennel Street Bakery, his cell phone rang.

"Chief Harris."

"Chief, good morning. It's Sam Snell."

"Good morning, Detective."

"I just wanted to let you know that I won't be over today. We have some new assignments from the weekend that I have to check on, but I do plan to try and interview your councilman again."

"He's still not talking?"

"No, but he's been too angry to reason with. I'm hoping he's better today."

"Anything I can do over here to help you out?" Conrad stopped on the sidewalk to finish the conversation before going into the bakery.

"No, nothing unless I can get something out of Langley. Any information you run across though, I'd appreciate your input. We still don't have a coroner's report. I'm hoping it provides some leads."

"Maybe it will come today. Call me if you need me."

"Thanks, Chief."

Conrad pocketed his phone and pulled open the bakery door to glide in on the cinnamon scent.

"Hey, Chief." Conrad waved to his morning gang and saw Bert Miller was already there shoveling a bear claw in his mouth. Bringing his own coffee mug each morning made him feel obligated to purchase something from the bakery, but he headed for the group before exploring the counter.

"Bert, did I miss the update? How did the neighborhood party go?" Conrad pulled over a chair from a nearby table.

"Pretty good. Joyce wants us to start having regular get-togethers out there. We've got a good group of neighbors." Bert folded his napkin and reached for his coffee.

"Anybody say they wanted to form an HOA?" Ned Carey asked.

"We took a vote, and two people are unsure. Everyone else voted no."

"Who are the two?" Ned nodded to the waitress that offered to fill up his coffee cup.

"Don't know." Bert shrugged. "It was a secret ballot. I just know that I can't go to Miriam and say we have a collective opinion now. I was hoping to go to her and tell her no one was attending her meeting, but now it looks like we'll have to go through the motions and let her have her say."

"Did Arlene Emery come to your party?" Conrad said in a lowered voice.

"You know about that, too? Geeze, I'm the last to know. I hadn't heard that Hobart bought a lot out there. Joyce just found out Saturday. We didn't invite her, but I didn't feel it was right to call her right now. What with everything going on, Joyce said it's a bad time. I'm sure Miriam invited her, and she'll have a chance to participate tonight if she wants."

"She's probably got a lot of other things on her mind," Ned said. "Any updates on the investigation?"

"It's not my case." Conrad scooted his chair back so he could prop his ankle on his knee. "I know just what you read in the paper today."

"Shocked me." Ted Parish shook his head and exhaled loudly. "You think you know people!"

"He's not convicted yet, Ted. Don't send him to the chair yet." Ned Carey laughed. "They're just talking to him. Knowing him, he's not cooperating."

Conrad nodded. It was unfortunate, but everyone's opinion of Larry Langley had been greatly damaged by his recent antics around town.

"I certainly hope Larry didn't do it." Bert slurped his coffee. "Apparently, Miriam and Hobart have some bad blood, too. Richard Tyner told us Saturday that he saw Miriam and Hobart in a screaming match last week. You know, Hobart's farm borders Richard's backyard. He said he's never had any problem with that at all. He didn't know what they were fighting about but voices were raised, and Miriam was in her hostile stance." Bert chuckled. "I don't know what else to call it, but you can see Miriam's anger from a distance."

Conrad nodded. He knew the body language well.

"It would make sense for Hobart to buy a lot right there next to the Tyners. He could walk out his back door in the morning and be at his farm." Bert checked his watch. "Pretty convenient."

"But he owns that farm. Why not just build on that land?" Ted shrugged.

"Maybe he didn't plan to build on it at all." Conrad mumbled, not really speaking to anyone.

"I'll be glad when this election is over. Too much drama for me. I'm ready for Spicetown to go back to being the happy place I live." Ned Carey held out his coffee cup.

"I second that!" Ted Parish said as he tapped Ned's coffee cup with his own.

CHAPTER FOURTEEN

"Ned, thank you for calling me back." Cora was fortunate. Ned Carey, Spicetown city attorney, had always been on her side. They had battled many challenges with the City Council over the years when they had tried to strong arm change for selfish reasons. Someone had to keep the council members in line, and it was usually Ned and Cora Mae.

"Of course, Cora. How can I help you?"

"I've been doing some research and I just want clarification of what I think I understand."

"Okay."

"If Larry wins the election tomorrow, he will retain his council seat as long as he isn't convicted of a crime. Is that correct?"

"That's correct."

"If Hobart wins tomorrow, the council has thirty days to appoint someone for that position and then we will have a special election after the first of the year. Is that right?"

"That's the way I read it. I'm sure we'll have to consult with the state during the process, but that about sums it up."

"Okay, I just needed confirmation that I was interpreting it correctly." Cora Mae frowned and studied her notepad.

"Do you think Larry will win?"

"I haven't the foggiest idea." Cora chuckled. "I can see folks feeling they can't vote for Hobart now. Will they switch their vote to Larry? Will they abstain from voting for that race? I could see it going either way. I wish they would write-in someone, but I don't know that people think to do that."

"Oh, you'll probably get a few that will write their own name in there." Ned huffed. "As long as they don't write in mine, I guess that's okay."

Cora laughed. "I can see a possibility that the council would appoint Larry to stay even if he loses. That might be a public relations problem though."

"I don't think Larry has the alliances he once did on the council. I think his behavior has burned some bridges. The rest of the council has to run for election in two years, too. They won't want to be labeled as a Langley supporter. Gordon Little might recommend him, but I don't think he can get a majority vote."

Cora Mae smiled. She had hoped that was the sentiment. "I'm curious about who they would appoint. I just don't have any idea where they stand."

"I could see Tom Womack recommending Ted Parish or Rick Manning. Gordon Little would probably support Rick Manning, too."

"Ted might have a hard time doing that job along with running the drugstore." Cora could see an insurance salesman fitting in well with the others, but it was odd that Rick Manning's name kept popping up lately.

"I don't think Ted wants it," Ned said.

"Hmm. Well, we don't have long to wait. The election is almost here. Thanks, Ned. Talk to you soon."

§

Officer Gwen Kimball appeared at Conrad's office door. "Chief, I'm getting ready to go out on patrol. Is it okay if I take Briscoe with me?"

"Yeah, I guess. You'll have to get his seatbelt out of my car. He rides in the front seat, but I hook his harness into a clip that connects to the seat belt."

"Okay, I'll get it."

Conrad walked to the dispatch cubicle and waited for Georgia to finish her call.

"Hey, Chief."

"Georgia, I just wanted to let you know I got a couple of messages to call Paulie Childers back at the Spicetown Star and I'm ignoring those. I know he just wants a statement on Langley's arrest, and

I can't make one. I've left him voice mails telling him he has to call the sheriff's office to get a statement. If he calls again today, please tell him that for me."

"Sure, Chief. The mayor called earlier when you were on the phone. She said to tell you she was going to lunch at the Caraway Cafe if you wanted to join her."

"Thanks, Georgie. I've got a few calls to make first."

Conrad stretched his arms up over his head before sitting back down at his desk. He was anxious today. Someone should be doing something about the Emery case, and it didn't seem like Paxton was taking it seriously. He was itching to read the coroner's report, but knew even if it was done, it wasn't his place to call over for it. He had hoped he might be invited to interview Larry or sit in with Snell when he interviewed, but the offer had not been extended. He wanted to be able to give Arlene some information other than nothing was being done. Larry would be released tomorrow if they didn't charge him.

Conrad reached for the phone and decided he had to do something.

"Miriam? This is Chief Harris. I had a couple of questions I'd like to ask you about Hobart Emery."

"And why would you be asking questions about Hobart?"

"I'm assisting the sheriff's department with interviews. Can you tell me about your relationship with Hobart Emery?"

"Now, Conrad. You're going to have to be more specific. I've known Hobart Emery for forty years. What is it you want to know?"

"Did the two of you get along?"

"Most of the time." Miriam huffed. "I don't get along with anybody all of the time."

"I understand you recently had a business deal with Hobart. He purchased a lot in your subdivision. Did you get along during that transaction?"

"Yes. Hobart bought a lot."

"Miriam, it was reported that you and Hobart were arguing last week. What was your argument about?"

"Who said we were arguing? We were just talking. He was out at his farm and I was in the subdivision waiting for a young couple who wanted to see the lots for sale. I walked over and talked with him for a couple of minutes. That's the last time I saw him."

"Specifically, what were you talking about? What was said?" Conrad regretted doing this by phone. Miriam was so evasive that it helped if he could look her in the eye.

"I asked him if he'd changed his mind about the lot he bought."

"Changed his mind?" Conrad sighed. "Please be specific. What were you referring to when you asked him this?"

"Hobart bought the lot a couple of months ago and I thought he and Arlene were going to build a house. A few weeks ago, I found out that he plans to move a couple of single wide trailers onto that lot and hook them up to the farm utilities for his farmhands to live in."

Conrad leaned back in his chair. "That's why you were hoping the other residents would vote for a homeowners association."

"I was hoping to change his mind."

"But you knew you wouldn't be able to sell the remaining lots with trailers sitting in the back of your subdivision." Conrad smiled. This may be a game changer for Bert Miller.

"I was trying to help the others that have built out there. They won't want to live with the eyesore of trailers next to their nice homes."

Conrad chuckled. Miriam didn't fool him. "Okay, Miriam. So, you and Hobart talked about it last week. Did your conversation change anything?"

"No. Hobart Emery was a hardheaded man. He did say he hadn't made up his mind for certain and hadn't talked to the farmhands yet, but he told me it was his lot to do with as he pleased."

"I understand your response to guide the homeowners to unite against it, however, wouldn't it have been easier to just send them a letter that said that?" Conrad shook his head. So much stress was caused for nothing, but that really had nothing to do with Hobart's death. "Never mind. Did you have any further contact with Hobart by phone or in person?"

"No. I walked away and he got in his truck. That's all there was to it."

"Did you by any chance notice if he had anything in the back of his truck?" Conrad thought those yard signs might have been visible.

"I didn't notice. If there was, it wasn't sticking up high enough for me to see."

"Thank you, Miriam. I'll write this up for the sheriff's office. If Detective Snell has any follow-up questions, he may give you a call."

"Fine." Miriam hung up without a goodbye, but that was usually her way.

Conrad debated about contacting Bert Miller. It wasn't really appropriate for him to share information gathered as a part of police investigation. Bert would hear about it this evening at the HOA meeting and the homeowners would have to make a decision on how they would go forward. It was best if he didn't get involved.

Grabbing his jacket, he walked out into the hallway and waved at Georgia Marks. "Going to lunch."

CHAPTER FIFTEEN

"Dot, if you get a minute, come sit with me." Cora had taken a table in the front window of the Caraway Cafe and Dorothy Parish was running around taking orders. Lunch time was always busy. Dorothy's husband, Frank, handled the grill and although Cora waved to him when she entered, his head was down tending to the orders.

"I'll be right out. Just need to get these orders in." Dorothy rushed by, whispered in a server's ear, and grabbed Cora's teapot of hot water. "Have you ordered yet?"

"No, but I'm going to wait a few minutes and see if the Chief shows up. I know you're busy, but I wanted to ask you about the meeting Saturday."

"Oh, I thought it went pretty well. Now that we have everyone's email address, Jason is going to make us a newsletter so we can communicate easily that way. Nobody has time for too many meetings."

"Yes, but I was curious if you know anything about the new girl, the new business. Had she contacted you before? She looks so familiar to me."

"You know her, Cora! She was Kelly Goins. Vaughn is her married name. I'm sure you had her in school. Her dad is Ken Goins. He sells used cars now, but he used to be a mechanic."

"Yes, I remember a Kelly Goins. Her mother is Mona. She's changed a lot. The girl I remember was plump and had dark hair."

"I don't know the Vaughn boy though. He must not be from here. She's working for Vicki at the bakery part-time right now." Dorothy waved at Conrad as he walked by the window. "The Chief's here."

"Were you surprised to see Jeff Wiggins there? I don't know anything about him, other than he worked at the quarry with Hobart."

"Hey, Chief." Dorothy stood up and motioned for Conrad to take her seat. "You know his wife." Dorothy rolled her eyes. "His ex-wife. She used to work at Louise's Beauty Shop. She did nails and her name was Twyla. A real tall girl with blonde hair."

"Oh, yes. I remember her. Very talkative."

"Yeah. She took Jeff's shirt <u>and</u> his socks in the divorce. It was a bad one and he's probably never going to financially recover. They've got three kids."

"That's awful." Cora said.

"I've got a pickup. Someone will be here shortly to take your order." Dorothy dashed off.

"Who were you talking about?" Conrad folded the menu and glanced at the chalk board near the door for the day's special.

"Jeff Wiggins. He worked at the rock quarry with Hobart. You know I've never been out there. I've never been inside a rock quarry."

"I don't think it's on too many people's bucket list. Not much to see."

"I think I should go out there and visit. The city has a contract with them. I need to see what the place looks like." Cora stirred sugar into her tea.

"I don't think they do tours, Cora." Conrad chuckled and Cora gave him a dismissive wave.

"I just want to see what's it's like."

"Whenever I've gone out there, I don't see much of anything going on. Once in a while they fill a truck, but that's about it. It's pretty desolate out there."

"I got the feeling at the Merchants Association meeting that Jeff feels like Hobart stiffed him. He got a raw deal in whatever arrangement they had. Hobart was a shrewd businessman, and Jeff was just a young man when he started out there. Hobart may have taken advantage of him."

"I talked to Miriam Landry this morning. She basically feels the same way. She had business dealings with Hobart, and he may have misrepresented his interests to her as well. It's not that he did anything wrong. He just outsmarted her."

"It might have been a lot of fun having him on the City Council." Cora smiled as the waitress walked up to take their order.

After the young lady left the table, Cora pointed a finger at Conrad. "I keep forgetting to ask you, did you catch Saucy's sign thief?"

"I haven't had much time to devote to that. The sheriff's office called the owner of the vehicle. He said the truck never left his driveway all night and his wife took it to work the next morning. I tried to call him back, but I've never been able to catch him in. I wanted to ask where his wife worked and try to talk to her since Saucy said it was a woman."

"Is the owner's name Vaughn by any chance?" Cora raised her eyebrows and leaned forward.

"As a matter of fact..."

"Well, the wife's name is Kelly Goins Vaughn and she's from Spicetown. She's working over at the bakery part-time, so she probably goes to work at four in the morning. When she was in high school, she was Lisa Langley's shadow. I would say they were best friends, but really it was one-sided. Kelly was more like a personal assistant to cheerleader superstar Lisa Langley. She was always with Lisa, but in the background. She worshiped the ground Lisa walked on and Lisa walked all over her. They may still be friends."

"Which would explain why she would help Larry by pulling up Hobart's signs and replacing them with Larry's."

"Yes. At least she'll be easy to find. I'm sure she's probably still working when you go in the bakery in the morning."

"Why do you know all this?" Conrad put his elbow on the table and propped his chin up with his hand.

"Kelly was at the Merchants Association meeting Saturday. Her husband owns a Burger Buddy restaurant in Paxton, and he wants to open one here in Spicetown. Maybe she was trading favors with Larry."

"I'll try to find out tomorrow morning." Conrad draped his napkin in his lap.

"I thought you might be in Paxton today. Any update on Larry?"

"Snell said he was going to try and interview him again today. They can't hold him much longer without charges, but Snell didn't invite me to come over. He probably doesn't know when he'll get a chance to do it. He's got a lot on his plate right now."

"I wish I knew what was going to happen tomorrow. I felt like Hobart had a good chance to win before he died, but now I don't know. I wish the Spicetown Star would print an article that explains what happens if you vote for Hobart tomorrow. I don't think people understand what happens next."

"They might. Paulie's been calling me for two days wanting a statement on Larry that I can't give. Maybe he'll use that empty space to print an article about the election."

"If there had been more time, I would have asked Ned to write something for Paulie, but..." Cora huffed.

"This too shall pass." Conrad chuckled as the waitress approached with their orders.

§

Gerald Landry stood at the door of the Chamber of Commerce and shook hands with each homeowner as they arrived. Miriam Landry had been president of the Chamber of Commerce for over twenty years, and she used the office space freely for her own endeavors. Her husband, Gerald, was an amiable man who was generally well liked among all. Miriam's biggest challenge was personal interactions. Gerald's biggest challenge was Miriam.

"Good evening, everyone." Miriam stood at a small lectern and faced the room of anxious homeowners. "I appreciate your interest in attending this evening. I promise I will keep the meeting short."

"Miriam," Bert said with a raised hand. "Most of us have discussed this and there isn't a lot of interest in forming an HOA."

"I know that many of you feel that way, but you may change your mind once you hear what I have to say." Miriam glared at Bert until he sat down in his chair. "Recently, I sold a lot in the back of the subdivision near the cul-de-sac to Hobart Emery. At the time, I was under the impression that Mr. Emery intended to build a home. Later, I discovered he planned to place one or two single wide trailers on the property for his farmworkers to live in. Currently, without any covenants, you cannot prevent this. I wanted to make you aware so you can take any action you may deem necessary."

"Are you kidding me?" Earl Lester looked over at Bert Miller.

Richard Tyner stood from his seat and waited until Miriam nodded her head. "Did Mr. Emery buy the lot next to mine?"

"He did." Miriam leaned forward on the lectern and looked at Richard waiting for a response, but Richard sat down. Soon the murmurs around the room began to grow louder as the guests began to talk among themselves.

"Since I don't have a ball in this game, I'll step out of the room and let all of you discuss it further. If you wish to enact some type of association, I have a template here on the table you can use as a guide. If you do not wish to go that route, please understand that I will be registering covenants for future sales in the subdivision, so this doesn't happen again."

"Wait," Earl Lester said. "Hobart is dead. Does his wife still plan to put those trailers there?"

"She hasn't made a decision yet." Miriam walked to the door and Gerald held it open for her as they stepped back into the reception area of the chamber office.

"You did a nice job tonight, dear." Gerald patted Miriam on the back. It was a rare sight to see his wife humble and helpful. Altruism was not a common motivator for Miriam's actions.

"I'm not going to let them blame this on me. They'll all have a fit if trailers start rolling in. The whole cul-de-sac will be a loss because I won't have any more buyers if Arlene goes through with Hobart's plan. It's hard enough to look at that farm back there. Trailers are the last thing I need."

"I know, dear." It had been a nice change of character, but it was short-lived.

CHAPTER SIXTEEN

"Good morning, Mayor." Amanda Morgan stopped typing and turned in her chair. "Did you already vote this morning?"

"No. It looked pretty busy, so I'll sneak out later and do that." Cora took her coat off and walked into her office.

Amanda came to Cora's doorway. "Mr. Salzman told me to tell you hello. He stopped in earlier. I don't think he needed anything."

"Saucy must have gotten an early start today. I see you've already voted." Cora pointed to her own lapel and then at Amanda's sticker on her sweater.

"Yes, thank you. I forgot they put that on me. I stopped on my way to work."

"I do hope people still vote. I know it's confusing right now, but I'm worried that the Hobart supporters will just opt to not vote at all and that would be unfortunate."

"They were talking about it on the radio this morning. I was listening in the car and callers were asking the radio station what would happen if Hobart wins. I hope someone who does know the answer calls in and tells them. That might help. I explained it to Bryan and my parents last night. They were all thinking that Larry Langley would automatically get another term."

"See," Cora said shaking her finger. "That's what I'm afraid is going to happen. I asked Paulie Childers to put something in the newspaper about this."

"My dad said he wasn't going to vote because one of his patients told him a vote for Hobart was a wasted vote. I think it's the talk of the town."

"You explained it all and now he's planning to vote, right?"

Amanda nodded.

"What about your mother? I'm sure it's been talked about at the beauty shop. She might be able to help spread the word."

"You know my mother is famous for spreading the word." Amanda chuckled. "She loves having a scoop to share so I know she'll tell everyone she can."

"There's just not enough time. We didn't have enough time to make sure everyone understood how the law is set up."

"Maybe you should call the radio station to see if they got the answers they needed this morning."

Cora frowned. "It really shouldn't come from me. Maybe I'll give Ned Carey a call and see if he will contact them." Cora glanced at the clock.

"He's probably at coffee right now. I'll wait a little while."

Amanda nodded and turned to walk back to her desk.

"Oh, Mandy. I keep forgetting to ask you, did you know Kelly Goins when you were in school?"

Amanda leaned on the door frame. "I know who she is. She's younger than me. She was Lisa Langley's friend."

"Yes, I had heard that. She was at the Merchants Association meeting Saturday. She married a man named Aaron Vaughn and right now she's living in Paxton, but her husband wants--"

"He's the Burger Buddy guy!" Amanda pointed her finger at Cora. "He introduced himself to me that day he came to the council meeting. Kelly wasn't with him, but he told me he wants to open a Burger Buddy in Spicetown."

"Yes, he presented a proposal to the council that day, but he hasn't made application yet. The big issue that was missing from his presentation was the location. He never told us where he planned to put his business. I don't know if he has plans to rent an existing storefront or whether he's building a structure. I looked and he doesn't own any property here in town in his own name. The location might make a difference to some of the council members. Having a franchise fast-food place in our downtown is something we've never allowed before, but if he was building somewhere away from the downtown, it's possible they might approve it."

"When he introduced himself, he did say he was thinking of applying after the first of the year. He said he was just here to meet the council and get a feel for whether they might accommodate his expansion."

"Hmm, maybe he wanted to wait until after the election." Cora stared off across the room.

§

"Good morning, Vicki. Is your new girl, Kelly Vaughn, working today?" Conrad looked in the glass case at the pastries on display.

"Kelly? Yeah, Chief. She's in the back. Do you know Kelly?"

"Actually, no. We've never met, but I needed to ask her some questions. Can you tell me what time she gets off work today? I don't want to interrupt your busy morning. I'll just come back later when it's more convenient."

"Has she done something wrong?" Vicki whispered as she looked over her shoulder. "You can tell me."

"I don't know yet. I do need to ask her a few questions, but I'd prefer you not mention it to her." Conrad winked.

Vickie picked up a white bag and grabbed some tissue paper. "What can I get you today?"

"I'll take a bear claw," Conrad said.

Vickie handed Conrad his bag as he felt his phone vibrate. "She gets off at noon. Mums the word."

Conrad waved at his buddies who were sitting near the window and walked out the front door to take the call.

"Chief Harris."

"Morning, Chief. It's Sam Snell."

"Good morning, Detective."

"Still no autopsy report, but there was trace blood on those yard signs I took. We're sending them to the lab."

"Hmm, no blood at the scene though." Conrad walked down the sidewalk to return to the office.

"No, but there was a scratch on his face. Who knows? It could be completely unrelated."

"Anything on the wood samples from the boat dock?"

"Not yet. I have to wait until the autopsy is complete. The reason I called, I wanted to see if you were interested in coming over to Paxton. We're going to be forced to release Langley tomorrow, but we've never gotten any statement from him. He won't cooperate. He keeps saying he won't talk to us without his lawyer present, but his lawyer has never shown up. I thought you might want to take a shot at it. Maybe he would talk to you."

"I could give it a try. Can it be tomorrow? I've got a few things going on today and the election today might make a difference. He might be afraid to talk before the vote." Conrad wanted to talk to Arlene and then needed to speak with the Vaughn girl today.

"Sure! I'll let the jail know you're coming. Let me know how it goes."

"Will do."

§

"Dorothy! Glad I caught you. I got your voice mail, but I'm not sure if I'm the right person for the job." Ned Carey tapped his pen on his desk pad. "Can you give me an example? What kind of legal help would the merchants in town be interested in? If it's just incorporation papers or something like that, yeah, I think I could handle that, but the city keeps me pretty busy."

"Thanks for calling me back, Ned. This was something I thought about, but I didn't plan to pursue it. Now that we've had the organizational meeting, it's come up again. It's something they're suggesting they could use."

"Did they give an example?"

"At the meeting, Jeff Wiggins brought it up. He said he could have used a legal opinion when he did a partnership agreement in the past. He felt like he got a raw deal because he didn't have any legal advice. My concern is that it could be a million things. My first thought was litigation. You know slip and fall claims are the scariest part of business ownership. Then there's injury claims from a worker, zoning issues... The possibilities are endless."

"Yeah." Ned took a deep breath. "I don't mind offering a discount for services to merchants in town if we define the type of service. I can't leave it open ended unless they would be satisfied with just a referral. I wouldn't mind hearing their concern and referring them to an attorney that specialized in what they needed."

"You would be okay with doing incorporations?"

"Yes, I can do that. Partnerships might be a bit trickier. There are two sides to that, and both probably need their own representation. I know what Jeff Wiggins is talking about because I reviewed his agreement with Hobart Emery years ago. Hobart hired me and I represented his interests, not Jeff's. It takes two to tango." Ned chuckled. "I don't want to get in between anybody."

"Oh, I can understand that."

"As for the personal injury stuff, that's better off handled by a firm that specializes in that area. I wouldn't want to take that on."

"Okay," Dorothy said with a huff. "How about we put you down as offering Spicetown merchants a reduced-price legal consultation. That way you can evaluate what they want and either offer them service or a referral to someone else. Would that work?"

"That should work!"

CHAPTER SEVENTEEN

"Connie! What are you up to on this fine election day?" Cora smiled at her own jovial greeting. She knew Conrad was probably scowling.

"Well, I'm on my way out to see Arlene Emery and I was calling to see if you wanted to tag along." Things always went better with grieving widows when Cora accompanied him.

"Sure! I haven't talked to her since Saturday. Today might be a tough day regardless of whether Hobart wins or not. Seeing his name on the ballot can't be easy on her."

"I'm pulling around back now."

"Okay, I'll be right out." Cora jumped up and pulled her handbag from her drawer. "Amanda?" Cora slipped her arm in her coat. "I'm going to run out to Arlene Emery's house with the Chief."

"Okay." Amanda nodded. "Is Mrs. Emery doing okay?"

"I haven't talked to her since Saturday. She's struggling, but that's understandable."

"It is."

"If I can talk the Chief into stopping, I may try to vote while I'm out."

"Good idea. I'll see you later."

Cora dashed down the back hall and out the employee exit door to Conrad's car.

"What's gotten you into such a cheery mood?" Conrad scowled as Cora climbed into the car.

"Well, I just got off the phone with Dorothy Parish. She's wrangled your old friend Ned Carey into representing the Merchants Association. Dot is definitely the right woman for the job."

Conrad chuckled. "Ned's a soft touch. He grumbles a bit, but he likes to help."

"They've cut a deal, so she's happy. She also told me that Ned represented Hobart Emery on the partnership deal at the rock quarry. Did I tell you his partner was at the Merchants Association meeting and he complained that he got a bad deal with the partnership? Apparently, Ned drew up the documents for Hobart and Jeff didn't get anyone to represent him."

"Hmm. Sounds like he was asking for someone to take advantage of him then."

"He was young. He probably thought Hobart would be fair." Cora hummed. "He didn't know Hobart well enough."

"Hobart was a businessman and the partnership was a business deal. It was Hobart's livelihood, and he did Jeff a favor letting him in."

"I wonder if he feels that way. He seemed a little bitter at the meeting."

"There's Hobart's pup." Conrad pointed at the black Labrador that raced across the yard toward the car as he pulled into the driveway. "I think his name is Jet."

"What a pretty boy!" Cora Mae scrambled out of the car to pet Jet as Arlene opened the front door.

"Hi, Chief. So glad you came along too, Cora." Arlene waved. "Come in."

Conrad held the door open for Cora and followed her into the living room.

"Coffee or tea? I've got both here." Arlene walked into the kitchen.

"I'll take some tea, dear. The wind is a bit chilly today." Cora followed Arlene into the kitchen.

"I hope it's not too cold to vote." Arlene smiled. "I haven't been myself yet, but I know I need to go vote for my husband today. It sounds silly. I know my vote won't count, but it's something I need to do."

Cora squeezed Arlene's shoulder and gave her a sideways hug. "It does still count. If Hobart wins, the council will select a replacement. Larry doesn't win by default. That's not how the law is written."

Arlene leaned back and looked at Cora. "Really? I didn't know that. I just thought it would be like an uncontested election or re-election for Larry."

"Towns have different laws, but I've already talked to Ned about it. He seemed pretty certain."

"I'm glad you told me. It will give me the motivation to get out of the house today. I'll definitely go cast my vote." Arlene handed Cora her cup and they returned to the living room.

"Chief, do you have any news for me yet?" Arlene sat down on the couch across from Conrad. "I haven't heard anything from the coroner."

"No, not yet. I spoke with the detective this morning and they don't have the report yet. I'm sorry."

Arlene sighed. "I'm anxious to make arrangements for his funeral, but I'm also dreading it. Do you know what I mean?" Arlene looked at Cora. "I guess I just need something to do."

"I hate to bother you," Conrad said as he crossed his ankle over his knee. "I just wanted to ask you a few questions on things I'm not sure about."

"Certainly, Chief. I'm happy to help any way that I can."

"First, tell me about the boat. How long had Hobart had the boat and was it always kept at the rental docks?"

"He bought that boat four years ago, but he always had a fishing boat. He loved to fish, and he never brought the boat home. He rented the lifts and stored the boat at the lake in the winter. He said it was easier." Arlene shrugged.

"Did you ever go along with him when he fished?"

"Years ago, but not in a long time. I was never really interested in it. He could always find a fishing buddy if he wanted one."

"So, he fished with other friends? Who usually went with him?"

"Oh, he used to fish with Bing." Arlene pointed at Cora Mae. "He went out with Jeff Wiggins, his partner at the rock quarry, for several years, too. Jeff didn't have a boat of his own, so Hobart took him along. He fished with Ted Aldridge on occasion and our pastor off and on, but the last few years he seemed to like going alone."

"And he was planning to go alone Friday?" Conrad pulled his notepad from his pocket.

"I assumed so. He didn't mention meeting anyone else." Arlene took a sip of her tea.

"You mentioned his partner, Jeff Wiggins. What can you tell me about that business arrangement? Is Jeff the full owner of the quarry now?"

"Oh, yes. He bought Hobart out and he is full owner now." Arlene smiled weakly. "He's had a lot of trouble these last few years." Arlene cringed. "Family troubles. Poor man."

"Yes, I know he's gone through a difficult time," Cora said. "I'm surprised he was able to buy Hobart out at all. I'm sure he's suffered financially."

"Oh, yes," Arlene exclaimed. "Mercy! The tales he would tell! I know he couldn't pay Hobart all at once, but they worked something out, so Jeff makes regular payments toward a loan. It's very complicated and I don't claim to fully understand it, but there was a fund set up when they became partners and that fund was supposed to pay retirement benefits, but because of Jeff's troubles, they put the money into an annuity, which is something like life insurance I'm told. Anyway," Arlene waved her arms. "It's supposed to pay me a monthly amount for living expenses. Rick Manning is handling all of it and at least he understands it." Arlene chuckled.

"Arlene, Rick isn't a financial adviser." Cora scooted to the edge of her seat and leaned forward. "He isn't licensed to handle funds for anyone. He is just an insurance salesman."

"Oh, he's got a broker's license and these funds are coming from some type of policy that he sold to them. That's why he's involved."

"Did Hobart also have life insurance?" Conrad thought he had been told that Arlene was getting insurance.

"He had insurance through work, but it was payable to Jeff, until Jeff had all these troubles. Rick said that was when they changed it to have it go into this annuity account. That's what the payments come from, you see. Instead of all at once, they come monthly. Hobart thought that would be easier to manage and better for tax purposes."

"Did Hobart tell you that?" Cora sat up straight. "Or did Rick tell you that?"

"Hobart and I didn't discuss things like we should have. I regret that, but he always said he would make sure I was taken care of and I trusted him."

"It sounds like perhaps now you are trusting Rick Manning, not Hobart." Conrad put his foot down and leaned back. "Do you have any documentation from Rick to support what he's telling you?"

"Oh, no Conrad, but it's nothing to worry about. I'm sure it'll be fine. Did you find out about those yard signs? The detective said there were yard signs in Hobart's boat. I can't imagine why they would be there. Hobart kept all of those at the farm."

"The signs they found were Larry's signs. Did Hobart have any of Larry's signs at the farm?" Conrad cleared his throat. "Are there any signs here at the house? Maybe in the garage?"

"Larry's! Hobart didn't have any of Larry's signs. That can't be right." Arlene shook her head.

"Do you mind if I look around the garage before we leave? Maybe someone else put them there."

"Go right ahead, Chief. Feel free to look around. I've never seen any signs at the house. Hobart told me they were stored in one of the barns out at the farm, and I know Ted Aldridge was helping him deliver them. Ted can show you."

"Did Hobart have any enemies, Arlene?"

Arlene flinched as if she had been struck.

Conrad leaned forward with his elbows on his knees. "Most businessmen have disagreements and argue from time to time. Anyone in particular that Hobart had difficulties getting along with or anyone who had negative feelings about Hobart?"

"Larry." Arlene shrugged. "Hobart argued some with Ted Aldridge, but Hobart was a stern taskmaster. I wouldn't call Ted an enemy. Hobart fired a number people over the years from the quarry and the farm. He's had arguments with all of them, but there's no one I would label an enemy necessarily."

"Okay, I'll check around outside for you. I don't want to keep you any longer." Conrad slipped his notepad into his coat pocket. "I know you need to get out and vote."

Arlene smiled. "Yes, I'm so glad to hear that my vote will count. I'm definitely going to go do that. Thank you, Cora."

"Arlene, if you could do me one favor," Cora said. "Please ask Rick Manning to provide you with copies of all these funds and whatever agreements that were signed. I know Ned Carey helped Hobart with the partnership agreement and Ned needs to look over this paperwork and make sure it's being processed correctly. I would hate to see you held liable or get in trouble with the IRS. Let Ned give you a legal opinion. You should really have copies of your own. What if something happens to Rick?" Cora held her palms up. "Will you do that for me?"

"I will, Cora. I'll ask him the next time I talk to him."

"Thank you," Cora said as she stood and picked up her coat. "I need to go vote now myself before the day gets away from me."

Conrad tipped his hat to Arlene and Cora Mae gave her a hug. "You call me if you need me."

"I will, Cora. I promise."

CHAPTER EIGHTEEN

"So, I take it you haven't voted?" Conrad backed out of Arlene's driveway, watching to make certain that the black Labrador Jet wasn't in the way. "Do you need me to run you by the poll?"

"I haven't, but I can go later. You need to get up to the bakery before Kelly slips through your fingers."

"I voted early this morning. There weren't too many people around. I hope that doesn't mean that the turnout is going to be low."

"They're probably just sitting at home wondering who they're supposed to vote for when neither man is available."

"Larry should be out tomorrow unless they aren't telling me everything. What do you know about Rick Manning?" Conrad turned the police radio down when it began to chatter.

"I know he's not someone you let plan your finances. Rick worked for ten years at a tire store. When that closed, he got a job selling insurance. Neither of those things qualifies him to invest Arlene's money. I don't know who has convinced

Arlene that Rick can handle that. I can't believe it was Hobart."

"That's probably a question we should have asked. I may try to contact Rick in a day or so and see if he gives me a song and dance. I want to talk to Larry first and give Arlene a chance to make some decisions. I'm getting the impression she really doesn't know what she has or what she's going to do."

"She seems a bit in limbo, but you feel like someone cut off your right arm when these things happen. I always thought I knew what was going on in my life with Bing until he was gone. Then I found out there were a lot of little things he handled for us that I didn't get involved with. You take that type of thing for granted when you've been together for years."

"I'm hoping Snell is still going to do some follow-up. Having the coroner's report will hopefully open some doors. If it comes back a blank, the sheriff's office may just drop it. Write it up as an accidental drowning and be done."

"I think that's what most people think it was. Arlene has not mentioned it and I don't know what the detective told her, but I find it a little odd that she hasn't even speculated about whether it was an accident or murder."

"She hasn't had much to say about Larry either," Conrad said. "I thought she'd ask about his arrest." Conrad glanced over at Cora. She was staring straight ahead, but her forehead was etched with worry lines. "Everyone handles things differently, though."

"True. True." Cora nodded. "You can just drop me off out front."

"I'm going to talk with Kelly and then head directly to Paxton."

"Well, good luck." Cora opened the car door and then looked back. "I'll talk to you later."

Conrad pulled the door to the Fennel Street Bakery open and marveled at how different the atmosphere was without the breakfast crowd. The tables shined and the white countertop was spotless, but the scent of baking was still in the air. Without any customers, the front register was empty, and Conrad walked to the end of the counter to peek into the kitchen.

"Vicki! Are you back there?"

"Hey, Chief." Vicki walked out wiping her hands on a towel. "Sorry. I was just washing my hands."

"Is Kelly Vaughn here?"

Vicki nodded and looked over her shoulder.

"I thought I'd just talk to her here." Conrad looked around the lobby. He didn't want to be overheard in case someone walked into the bakery, but everything seemed out in the open.

"You can go around this corner here." Vicki pointed as she walked out from around the counter. "We have a small table and chairs back here that employees use for break."

"Perfect." Conrad looked at his watch. "I'll wait until she's off."

Vicki gave him a dismissive wave. " I'll go get her."

Conrad pulled out the chair and removed his coat. Sending a quick text to Georgia Marks in dispatch, he sat back to wait on Ms. Vaughn.

"Did you want to see me?" Kelly Vaughn stood in the doorway of the kitchen with wide eyes. She had a hairnet on her head and rubber gloves on her hands, but she was a slimly built young woman that may very well be Saucy's thief.

"Are you Kelly Vaughn?" Conrad stood up. "I'm Chief Harris."

Kelly nodded meekly.

"Can you have a seat? I have a few questions I need to ask you."

"About what?" Kelly sat down and frowned.

Conrad leaned back in his chair and cleared his throat. "About the yard signs. I'd like you to tell me why you were doing it."

"I don't know what you're talking about." Kelly's breathing was shallow, and she tried to keep her face expressionless, but Conrad could see nerves.

"Yes, you do. You were going around and pulling up Hobart Emery yard signs and replacing them with Larry Langley signs. There's no reason to try and deny it. The residents watched you. They turned in your license number and described you. They're ready to file trespassing and theft charges on you. I want to know why. Why would you do something like that? What is Larry Langley to you?"

"Nothing. I didn't hurt anything." Kelly pulled off her hairnet and tossed it on the table.

"You went on people's property in the dark and removed signs that they asked to be placed there and you stuck a sign in their yard that they didn't want. Did you think they wouldn't notice?" Conrad leaned forward. "I can tell you that they did mind very much."

"I wanted to help Larry Langley win. He said he'd help my husband and the signs were the only way I knew to help." Kelly tossed the rubber gloves on top of the hairnet.

"Okay, what kind of help did Larry offer to give your husband?"

"It wasn't like that." Kelly began to fidget in her chair and twist her hair behind her ear.

"What was it like? Start at the beginning. I don't have all day."

Kelly looked down at the table and Conrad waited.

"Let's just go back to the station. My car is out front, and you can sit in a cell until you decide what your story is. I have other places to be." Conrad didn't want to bother with this, but he knew the residents of Dill Seed Drive were going to demand results.

"You're going to arrest me?"

"I don't have any choice if you don't have anything to say."

"I guess I need an attorney." Kelly raised her eyes with a stern expression.

"That's your choice." Conrad stood up and pushed his chair in. "Please stand and place your hands behind your back." When Kelly didn't stand, Conrad grabbed her elbow and pulled her up.

"It was nothing, really. It's not a big deal! I can't believe you're doing this."

"Believe it." Conrad steered Kelly to the front door of the bakery and glanced over his shoulder at Vicki, who stood bewildered behind the counter. "Thanks, Vicki. See you tomorrow."

Conrad guided Kelly to the back door of his squad car and walked around his car to slide into the front seat. Pulling away from the bakery, he made a U-turn on Fennel Street to head back to the police department and saw Harvey Salzman standing on the sidewalk in front of the Caraway Cafe. Harvey's stunned expression made Conrad smile. Saucy always wore his emotions on his face without any thought to conceal them. Conrad waved at Saucy and then grabbed his police radio.

"Georgie, is Kimball in the office?"

"Yeah, Chief."

"I'm pulling into the parking lot. Can you send her outside?"

"Sure, Chief."

Conrad pulled into a parking place in the front of the police station so the office cameras would record their movements and waited for Officer Gwen Kimball to approach the car.

"Hey, Chief."

"Can you put her in holding for me? I need to get to the SO."

"Sure, Chief."

"Pat her down, read her rights and give her paper so she can write a statement if she wants. I'll be back to question her later."

§

"Amanda, did you see this?" Cora walked out to Amanda's desk with a folder in her hand. "Burger Buddy has filed an application for a business license."

"Yes." Amanda smiled. "Laura brought it in shortly after you left with the Chief this morning. She said it came in the mail today."

"I guess he decided not to wait until the first of the year."

Amanda shrugged. "With Hobart's death, maybe he feels the election is over."

"My thoughts exactly, but that is far from the truth. Oh, speaking of that, I need to go vote."

"You didn't get a chance to do that when you were out with the Chief?"

"No, he had voted already, and he had other things he needed to get done today. I think I'll run and do that right now. After I vote, I'm going to visit the Spicetown Rock Quarry."

"The quarry?" Amanda made a sour face. "It stinks out there!"

"I've never been inside, and I've been thinking about it since Jeff Wiggins spoke at the Merchants Association meeting Saturday. I'm curious about it. I don't really know what they do."

"Okay," Amanda said with a smirk. "I don't think there is much going on out there, but I could be wrong."

"I remember years ago when Bing was mayor, he mentioned that they received a lot of complaints about the quarry. The folks living out within a mile or two of the place were calling and complaining about the blasting, the smell and the truck drivers flying down the road spilling gravel off their trucks. He would contact Hobart and try to work something out, but it was an active mine. I never hear anything about it anymore, but we still get our gravel from them."

"It's a lot bigger than it looks. I remember when I was in high school, I went out there one day with a friend. Her dad worked out there and she was taking him lunch. There's the main building there on Rosemary Road that you see when you drive by, but when you turn in, the road goes way back behind that building and that's where the quarry is. It's all fenced and locked. We had to stop at the gate and give her dad's lunch to the gate attendant. They wouldn't let us inside, but we could see it. It's huge and there are big piles of gravel all over the place with dump trucks and bulldozers. It's noisy, but it's way off the road in the middle of nowhere."

"Sounds exciting!" Cora grabbed her coat. "I'll be at the rock shop if anyone needs me."

Amanda chuckled as Cora waved goodbye.

CHAPTER NINETEEN

"He's been asking for you." Detective Sam Snell shook Conrad's hand.

"Really?" Conrad leaned back and furrowed his brow. "I never expected that."

"You two are acquainted, aren't you?"

"Yeah, but we're not buddies. I arrested his daughter last year and almost had to arrest him. We're not on the best of terms."

"Maybe he is just looking for a familiar face."

"Well, I brought that with me," Conrad said with a chuckle.

"He's over there." Detective Snell pointed to an interview room with a one-way mirror. "Holler if you need anything."

"Will do." Conrad looked through the window first. Larry was sitting with his elbows propped on the table. His fingertips massaged his temple, and his gaze was down, but Conrad could see the dark circles under his eyes. Even though it had only been a couple of days, Larry looked withered.

"Chief!" Larry jumped up from the table when Conrad opened the door to the interview room.

"Councilman." Conrad nodded. "Have a seat."

"There's no need to call me that anymore. I know that's over."

"The election isn't over yet. You may get out of here in time to vote. The Sheriff's Office just needs a statement from you. Why won't you talk to them? You could have been out Sunday night." Conrad threw his hands up in the air and shook his head.

"I knew I couldn't talk to them. They'd never understand what happened. It looks bad, I know, but I didn't kill Hobart."

"So, tell me. You were at the dock and Hobart arrived."

"Yeah." Larry nodded. "I was up on the road. I'd just hooked my boat up and pulled it out. He got out of his truck hollering at me. I don't know what he said. Then he starts laughing."

"Did you speak to him?"

"Not right away." Larry took a deep breath and blew it out. "You all think Hobart is this down home good old boy who seems so laid back and nice. That's not who Hobart Emery really is. You can ask anyone who has ever worked for him and they'll tell you. He's a back-stabbing manipulative old cuss, and he's played the whole town with his act."

"We'll get to that." Conrad waved his hand. "Let's just go through the motions first. Hobart is getting out of his truck and he's laughing. What happens next?"

"He asked me if I had a good time at the debate last night. I told him it wasn't a debate. It was supposed to be a chance for the people to get to know something about us. Then he laughed again and said that I'd shown everyone what a hothead I was."

"And did you respond?" Conrad couldn't see Larry letting something like that go.

" I told him that the people of Spicetown already know that, but they still don't know who he is. He just laughed again and told me I was an amateur."

"Were you on the dock or on land when this was going on?"

"I was on land. My boat was hooked up and I was getting ready to pull it out."

"Okay, he calls you an amateur. What did you say?"

"Nothing. I just went about my business. I didn't want to talk to him." Larry pushed back away from the table and crossed his arms over his chest. "He's a jerk, Conrad. The guy is a horrible human being, and nobody believes me."

Conrad held up his hand. "Let's stay on task here. What happened next? Did he ever walk up to you or did he just go to his boat?"

"He walked over to his dock as I was getting out of my truck. I had to secure some stuff in the boat before I could pull out on the highway. Hobart started yelling, telling me to get over there and get my stuff. I didn't know what he was talking about. I tried ignoring him, but he kept yelling and then he started toward me."

"Did he walk over to your truck?"

"No, he was waving his arms and ordering me to get over there. Finally, I walked over to his dock. That's when I saw he had my signs."

"Do you know how they got there?" Conrad raised an eyebrow.

"No! I sure didn't put them there. Why would I?" Larry threw both hands up in the air.

Conrad recognized the rise in Larry's voice and leaned back to slow things down. "Did Hobart ask you to remove them?"

"He told me to get them out of his boat. I told him to toss them up on the dock and I'd take them."

"Now, was it really that civil?" Conrad scoffed. "Was Hobart the only one yelling?"

"No, I was yelling, too. I admit it. I accused him of stealing those signs. He denied it, of course, but it's pretty obvious."

"Did Hobart toss the signs to you on the dock? Was there anything else on the dock?"

"No. He threw two of them at me. I had to step back to keep from being hit, but after that, he changed his mind. He started climbing out of his boat and saying that he was taking the signs. They were in his boat and they were his property now. He was going to take them out and sink them in the middle of the lake. I didn't need them anymore because I'll never be running for City Council again."

"Did you take the two that were on the dock?"

"I tried to. I picked one up but then he tried to grab it out of my hands."

"Tug of war?"

"Yeah, he kept twisting and tugging on it while he told me what a loser I was, and we wrestled over the sign for a minute."

"Did you hit him?"

"No." Larry shook his head. "I'm guilty of being a loudmouth, but I don't take shots at people, especially not old men. I wouldn't do that unless he swung on me first."

Conrad held up his hand and took a breath, hoping Larry would do the same. "Okay, so you're both wrestling to get the sign. Who wins?"

Larry smiled. "I let it go."

Conrad frowned.

"I'm sorry. It was funny. The old coot wouldn't turn loose of it, so I just let it go and he fell off the dock and into the lake."

"And you laughed at him?"

"Yeah, I did. He deserved it."

Conrad shook his head in disappointment. "Did you say anything to him?"

"He was still yelling at me. I told him I hoped he could swim, and I left."

"You left him in the water?"

"Yep, I sure did."

Conrad glared at Larry.

"Don't look at me that way. He was fine. He can swim and he was still yapping at me. I don't remember what he said, but it was just trash talk. I didn't say anything else to him. Well, maybe I told him he could keep the signs he stole, but then I walked off. I got in my truck and pulled my boat home."

"Did you see Hobart get back up on the dock?"

"No. I told you I walked away, and I didn't look back, but I could hear him."

"Are you sure he wasn't yelling at you to help him?"

"I'm sure. He was calling me names. He was clearly angry, not frightened."

"Do you know whether or not Hobart could swim?"

"I don't, but he's out on the lake by himself all the time. He talks about fishing a lot. It never entered my mind, but he could have yelled for help if he needed it. I was standing right there. I wouldn't have left a drowning man, Conrad."

"Okay, so you pull your boat and drive straight out Eagle Bay Road. Right?"

Larry nodded.

"You would have turned left and when you did that, did you look back down at the docks? Did you see Hobart?"

"If I did, I don't remember. I was angry myself, and frankly, I wasn't thinking about anything but getting out of there."

"Do you know what time this all happened?"

"No, not really. My wife might be able to tell you better than I could. She had to listen to me when I got home." Larry chuckled. "I just know it was morning."

"Okay, you're driving down Eagle Bay Road. What did you see? Did you pass anyone? See anyone in their yard? Wave at anyone?"

Larry frowned. "I waved at Hazel Linton when I pulled in, but I didn't see her when I left. I didn't look for her, though. I don't think anyone was outside. I passed Jeff Wiggins at the intersection of Eagle Bay and Rosemary Road. I passed Ernest Dorn at Clover Road. He honked at me. When I pulled into my street, I saw Pam Ritter on her porch across the street. That's all I can think of."

"That's helpful. Backup just a bit for me. What were you doing before you went to the docks?"

"Had breakfast with my wife and then went to get the boat."

"And after you got home, what did you do?"

"Told my wife what happened. My daughter and her boyfriend were there for a while, so they heard about it, too. After they left, I went out in the backyard and stored the boat in the pole barn and pruned some of the shrubs in the backyard. I was home all afternoon. Watched some television after lunch. Nothing exciting."

"Sit tight." Conrad stood up.

"Are you going to get me out of here?"

"I'm going to see if I can find out what's going on. I don't make the decisions on this. I'll be right back."

Larry slumped forward again with his head in his hands and Conrad pulled the door shut behind him.

"Have you been listening?" Detective Sam Snell was standing at the one-way mirrored window.

"Yeah. Why couldn't he just do that Sunday night? He was threatening to sue everybody he saw and raving like a mad man."

"I'm familiar." Conrad snorted. "I've seen that act myself. When I arrested his daughter last year, I thought I was going to be forced to lock him up, too."

"So, is he being straight with you?"

"Yeah, I think so." Conrad nodded. "He's too high strung and nervous to relay information this calmly if he was guilty of any wrongdoing. That's not to say he wasn't negligent if Hobart couldn't swim or drowned, but I don't think he had intent to cause bodily harm. It's just two old men acting like kids and it's been that way through the whole election."

Sam Snell chuckled. "I'm happy to cut him loose. He can go back to Spicetown and be your problem again."

CHAPTER TWENTY

"Hi, Chief. No, she went to vote and then out to the quarry. I don't really know when to expect her back."

"The quarry! The rock quarry? Why on earth..."

"She said she's been thinking about it and she's never been out there. She wanted to go see it."

Conrad growled. "That's the last place she needs to be. I'll try to call her cell. Thanks."

Conrad punched the buttons on his dashboard navigation screen and listened to the phone ring until the voice mail came on. "Cora, this is Conrad. Please call me as soon as you get this message, uh, unless you're still at the quarry. If you are, please get away from there first, and then call me. Thanks."

Before Conrad could disconnect his call, another call was coming in. "Chief Harris."

"Chief! It's Sam Snell. Are you already on the road? I was trying to catch you."

"Yeah, I'm on my way back. What's up?"

"We got an autopsy report, and it looks like I'll be back in Spicetown tomorrow."

"Oh, yeah?"

"Deputy Coroner York ruled it a suspicious death, possible foul play. Emery's fingers and nail beds are damaged. Seems like he may have tried to get out of the water, and someone stomped on his hands."

"Or whacked them with that oar." Conrad had worried about that oar on the dock. It would have made an excellent distance weapon.

"There are contusions to his head, too, but the prints on the oar don't belong to Langley. I've already had them run them."

"The oar may not have been there when Larry was on the dock with Hobart." Conrad frowned. "Did you catch the comment Larry Langley made about passing Jeff Wiggins on Eagle Bay Road when he left?"

"I did. Do you know Wiggins?"

"He used to be Hobart's business partner. Well, first he was an employee of the rock quarry and worked for Hobart for years, then they entered into a partnership. Hobart retired and Jeff runs the quarry now."

"Friend or foe?"

"I'm not sure," Conrad hummed. "I know recently Jeff indicated that he felt like Hobart took advantage of him in their partnership deal, but he's running the company on his own now. I don't know if there's any grudge there or not."

"Maybe we can get prints tomorrow when we interview him. I'll be over around nine in the morning if that's okay."

"Sure. I'll see you then."

Conrad tapped the redial button and called Cora's cell phone again. When she didn't answer, he called the office.

"Georgia, I'm on my way back to Spicetown. I need you to send a car out to the Spicetown Rock Quarry. I'm told the mayor is out there, but she's not answering her phone. I'm at least twenty minutes out. Can you send a car there to find her and tell her she is needed at her office?"

"Sure, Chief. No problem. Ted Aldridge was just here. He dropped off a list for you."

"Oh, yeah. Can you put that in an evidence bag for me? Thank you."

§

"Fascinating!" Cora Mae pulled off her hard hat and fluffed her hair as Jeff turned his truck into the front parking place by the plant office door. "I wish I had done this years ago. I wonder if my husband ever came out here. I don't recall him telling me about it if he did. Did you know George?"

"No, not personally. Back then I would have been back working in the quarry so I might not have known if he visited. Hobart was up front in the office then."

"I hope he was able to visit. He would have loved it, too. It's very noisy but amazing to see all the gigantic earth moving equipment."

"Some very serious equipment out there." Jeff opened his truck door.

"I'm so glad you keep this locked up. Someone could really get hurt in there if they didn't know what they were doing."

"I know people have tried to get in. Mostly teenagers, but we keep it pretty secure."

"Well, I should be getting back. City Hall will think I've gotten lost."

"Before you leave, I wanted to give you a souvenir of your tour." Jeff smiled. "Can you spare a minute to step back inside with me?"

"Well, I guess one more minute can't hurt. Sure." Cora pushed the truck door closed and straightened her sweater. Feeling a little disheveled, she walked around the truck to follow Jeff back in the office.

"Give me just a minute." Jeff was calling out to Cora from behind the counter somewhere, but she couldn't see him.

Cora strolled around the office and saw an inch of dust had settled on every surface. The magazines on the table were over a year old and the business cards on the counter still bore Hobart's name.

Jeff came around the corner just as the front door swung open and Officer Darren Hudson walked into the office lobby. "Here you go, Mayor."

"Darren! What brings you out to the quarry?" Although the quarry was called the Spicetown Rock Quarry, it was technically not within the city limits of town. Cora looked back at Jeff and saw that he held up a white ceramic coffee mug with the quarry logo printed on it.

"Mayor." Officer Hudson tipped his hat.

"That's lovely, Jeff! I love it. I'll keep it on my desk and when everyone asks about it, I'll tell them about my tour." Cora Mae chuckled. "Just drop it in my bag there if you would." Cora's large satchel handbag was on the counter between them and she held the handles apart. "Thank you!"

"Mayor, I'm sorry to interrupt. You're needed back at City Hall."

"Oh, my goodness. I told you I was going to get in trouble for being gone so long."

Jeff chuckled. "I'm glad you came by today."

"I am, too. Okay, Officer. I'm coming." Cora shuffled over toward the door and Officer Hudson pulled the door open to hold it for her. "Bye."

Cora jogged up beside Officer Hudson. "What's going on?"

"I don't know, ma'am. Georgia just told me to come out here and deliver that message from the Chief."

"The Chief, hmm. Okay, wait. Do you have an evidence bag in your car?"

“Yes, ma’am.”

Cora walked around the squad car when Officer Hudson opened the door and held her handbag open. “See that coffee mug? Can you put that in a bag for me and do whatever it is you do? You know, write something on it and give it to the Chief. It has Jeff Wiggins’ fingerprints on it, and he may need those.”

Slipping a glove on his hand, the officer lifted the mug and placed it in the evidence bag.

“Thank you, Darren. I’ll see you later.” Cora slid into her car and pulled out her cell phone. She saw two missed calls from Conrad and decided Darren’s visit had more to do with where she was than with the office needing her to return. She would listen to those messages later. Right now, she needed to leave before her police escort did, so she fastened her seatbelt and pulled out onto the road.

§

"Mrs. Vaughn," Conrad said as he entered the interview room with a nod of his head. "I'm Chief Harris. Shall we try this again?" Conrad had been surprised to learn that Kelly Vaughn had waited for his return without a sound. Officer Kimball said she had not asked a single question or made a phone call. She just sat in the cell and waited.

"Hi, Chief. Look. I really don't want to make a big deal of all this. If I offended anybody, I'm sorry. I just thought that I'd put out some signs on the main streets in town to help out my friend's dad. That's all there was to it. I didn't think anybody would care. It's just a sign and I only did it on the streets that get a lot of traffic."

"Like Dill Seed Drive and Sage Street." Conrad nodded.

"Yeah. I just wanted to help. I wasn't trying to hurt anybody. I don't see why it's such a big deal."

"I know you don't and that's part of the problem." Conrad scooted his chair forward. "You don't understand why these people feel violated by what you did. You think it was nothing. Have I got that right?"

"I don't think I should have been arrested for it!"

"Maybe you've never had anyone come onto your property and steal from you or sneak around in the dark while you sleep. It's a pretty creepy feeling to most folks. Maybe someday you'll grow up and understand that."

"That's not fair. I had to go early--"

"Right now, sitting here and telling me that what you did, which was property theft and trespassing, sends a clear message to me that you don't respect other people. Not to mention the violation these folks feel at how you thought it was perfectly fine to use their property for your own promotion. They don't support Larry Langley. If they did, they would have put the signs up themselves."

"I get it." Kelly held her hands up. "I wasn't thinking about all that."

"Some of these property owners are frightened by the thought someone was lurking around their house at night. Some are insulted by your brazen and inappropriate actions, and some are just plain angry."

"What am I supposed to do about it now? Tell me how to fix it."

"I'd say you have a lot of apologizing to do, but even that won't help if you can't correct the attitude. Maybe if you go door to door and personally apologize to these homeowners, they may decide to let it go. But if any of them decide they want to press charges, then you'll have to put your show on for the judge.

"Okay, I'll do that." Kelly stood up.

"Have a seat." Conrad turned his notepad around and placed a pen beside it. "I'll leave you in here for as long as you need to write out your statement. You make sure it covers what you did, when you did it and why you did it. If any of the residents decide to pursue this, understand that your statement will be filed along with charges for trespass and property theft. A warrant will be issued and a court date set. Do you understand?"

"Yes, Chief."

"Knock on the door when you're finished." Conrad walked out and locked the door.

CHAPTER TWENTY-ONE

"Coming," Cora Mae called out in a sing-song tone to match the doorbell. Scooting her slippered feet down the hallway, she laughed as her orange cat, Marmalade, jumped at her ankles in play. "Can't catch me."

Conrad held the pizza up as Cora opened the door.

"Hmm, smells good. Come on in." Cora reached for the pizza and saw papers on top of the box. "What's this?"

"Autopsy came back."

"Yum! Just what I wanted with dinner." Cora Mae's laughter bubbled out as she snaked around the hallway to the kitchen.

"Oh, sorry. I didn't even think about that." Conrad removed his hat and scratched his head.

"Of course, you didn't. Tea to drink?"

"Yeah, that's fine. I got your coffee mug." Conrad sat down at the kitchen table.

"I know. You think I'm crazy and maybe you don't need it, but if not, I'll take it back for my coffee. I just thought it might be something--"

"No, it was a great idea. In fact, it's exactly what I needed." Conrad reached down and rubbed Marmalade's head as she leaned against his shins.

"Really? Wow, I must be psychic. It sounds silly, but I know he was close to Hobart and I know they got on shaky ground. I'm still not certain where they stood despite asking him a million questions today. He just gives me an uneasy feeling. He's hiding something. He worked too hard at not answering me."

"He's hiding the fact that he went to the lake after Larry left."

"What? On my," Cora said as she placed the drinks down on the table.

"That's why I wanted you out of there today. He's just become a suspect."

"So, Larry is in the clear now? I didn't think he did anything wrong." Cora pulled her chair up to the table and passed Conrad a napkin before opening the pizza box. "Tell me everything."

In between bites, Conrad shared Larry's story of his encounter on the dock.

"Maybe this whole thing really is a bad accident." Cora dabbed at her mouth with a napkin. "I called Arlene tonight to check on her, but we didn't talk long. She said Ted was there for dinner. I told her I'd call her tomorrow. Whether Hobart wins this election or loses, tomorrow might be a tough day."

"Ted Aldridge?"

"Yes. I guess she invited him. She said they get along well."

"Hmm," Conrad said. "I wonder if he'll keep running the farm. I need to talk to him again, too. Except for Arlene, he's the only one that knew Hobart was headed for the lake Friday morning."

"Did you ask Larry about the signs?" Cora grabbed another napkin. "Saucy is going to need an update!"

Conrad chuckled. "I did. I asked him while they were processing him out of jail. He first said he didn't know Kelly Vaughn, but when I mentioned her maiden name, he changed his story. He said she was a friend of Lisa's, but she moved away. He didn't seem to know she was living in Paxton, let alone stealing signs for him."

"And does that match Kelly's story?"

"Well, that was a little messy. I had to arrest her this morning and let her sit in holding all afternoon before she decided to talk to me."

"Oh, mercy." Cora shook her head.

"Then she told me that Lisa Langley asked her to do it. Lisa said her dad would vote for Aaron's burger joint if he won."

"Did Larry deny this?" Cora raised an eyebrow.

"He did."

"I wouldn't have expected Larry to support a fast-food place, but he's not always predictable. How did these signs end up in Hobart's boat?"

"Kelly said she put the signs in the wrong boat because Lisa sent her a text saying her dad was coming out to the lake Saturday to get his boat. Lisa had been dropping signs in Larry's boat for Kelly to pick up when she needed them. She couldn't take the signs home, or her husband would get wind of what she was up to. When Lisa told her they needed to be moved, she dumped them in another boat. She thought no one would notice for a few days until she figured out what to do with them."

"She couldn't have been more wrong." Cora refilled her tea glass and offered some to Conrad. "Did you let her go?"

"I made her write a statement and told her to go down Dill Seed Drive and apologize to all the homeowners. If she did that to their satisfaction, maybe they wouldn't press charges."

"You better call Saucy tomorrow and warn him. He doesn't like surprises. He'll handle it better if he has time to prepare himself."

Conrad smiled. "If she plays her cards right, they will all probably forgive her as long as she's humble. She started out a little cocky with me and that kind of attitude won't work on Dill Seed Drive. Dean Teggers isn't going to tolerate being disrespected. He lost a night's sleep over that young lady." Conrad waved his hand in the air. "I had to hear the whole story."

"I can hardly wait to hear Saucy's report on this!" Cora Mae laughed.

"Now, tell me about your trip to the rock quarry." Conrad tossed his napkin on his plate. "I was calling to tell you Jeff was seen at the lake and Amanda tells me you're at the quarry. I couldn't believe it!"

"The quarry tour was actually quite interesting. I'd never been back in there behind the office before and I was shocked at how huge it all was. You know I love all that heavy equipment." Cora Mae giggled. "A dangerous place though. I'm glad they keep it locked up tight."

"What exactly were you trying to find out? Did you think he was involved?"

"No, I just know he was at one time pretty close to Hobart and he made it sound at the meeting like that wasn't the case anymore. I wanted that history. I wanted to know what happened between them."

"And did you find out?" Conrad pushed his chair back from the table and turned sideways.

"No, not really. He was very evasive about everything I asked. He told me that the partnership arrangement had been great at first, but in hindsight, he wasn't sure he would do it again. He mentioned that he was getting along better with his ex-wife now. He said they were working on things." Cora made air quotes. "It would probably be less expensive for him if they got back together."

"Did you get the impression that the business was in trouble?"

"No, not at all. He seemed pretty optimistic about it for the most part. He said Hobart's retirement was difficult, but that now the quarry was running smoothly." Cora picked up their plates and cleared the table. "Do you want to go sit in the living room where it's more comfortable?"

Conrad stood and followed Cora with Marmalade on his heels. "Hmm, that's not what I heard. I know some of the folks out on Lavender Lane said that when they tried to make appointments to get their footings poured for their new houses out there in Miriam's subdivision, Jeff told them he didn't have a working truck to do the job. He even referred Earl Lester to another business in Paxton. He did bring some loads of rock out a few times, but it was river rock that he bought south of here. It wasn't from the quarry. I was beginning to wonder if they were mining anything at all."

Cora gasped. "Really? Well, there were trucks everywhere today and piles of rock in all different sizes. I saw a lot of activity."

"Maybe something has changed. Earl and Bert called the quarry back in the spring. Something may have happened to change things for them in the last six months."

Cora propped her feet on the ottoman and crossed her ankles. "I have to admit, he made me uncomfortable today, but I can't say why, other than he was evasive, and that always makes me suspicious."

Conrad laughed and Marmalade jumped in his lap.

"He did tell me that he was thankful that Hobart brought him into this business, but he implied that he had not enjoyed working with Hobart. I think even though they were partners on paper, Hobart treated him like he was his assistant. Every time I tried to dig a little, he would tell me that he didn't know, that Hobart handled those things. Well, Hobart has been gone for a couple of years now. He has to know more than he's saying."

"Detective Snell is coming over in the morning and I'm sure we'll probably go out and talk with Jeff. I'll have to follow Snell's lead, but I would expect he will want to pull him into the office."

"So, what did the autopsy say? Did you get to talk to Alice?" Marmalade jumped up on the ottoman and curled around Cora's feet.

"It said there were contusions to his face and his hands. I didn't talk to anyone, but Deputy Coroner York wrote the report and Sam talked to him. He said there is evidence that someone may have kept Hobart from getting back up on that dock. There was a scratch on his face, but I think the lab is going to find that it's just from the sign hitting his cheek when Larry let go of it. It was nothing. The write-up said they found extensive bruising."

"The one time Hazel isn't paying attention..."

"The fingerprints might be the key to solving this. Larry said there were two signs on the dock when he left, and he didn't see any oar. When Sam and I got there, the signs were all in Hobart's boat but there was an oar on the dock. I'm thinking the killer may have used the oar that was left on the dock and picked up the signs to toss them in the boat. They've already printed the oar at the lab and told Sam that the prints don't belong to Larry. All we need is something to send for comparison. That's why your coffee mug souvenir was so perfect. I had Hudson drive it over to the Sheriff's office this afternoon so they can get it sent to the lab as soon as possible."

Cora sat up straight in her easy chair. "I knew you were going to need that!" Marmalade meowed in protest when Cora Mae and Conrad laughed.

CHAPTER TWENTY-TWO

"Morning, Chief." Officer Kimball peeked around Conrad's office door.

"Good morning."

"I just wanted to check and see if you needed me for anything more on that case at the lake. Are you still working on that?"

"The sheriff's office is," Conrad said. "Detective Snell is coming back over today. I think he's got a few interviews to do."

"I overheard some conversation last night about the Emery farm. It may not mean anything, but--"

"Come in." Conrad waved her toward the chairs across from his desk. "What did you hear?"

"Well, I walked down to Sesame Subs to get something for dinner last night. I decided to eat it there, since I was walking back, and some guys sat down at the next table."

Conrad nodded.

"Of course, I don't know who they are because I don't know anyone yet." Gwen Kimball shrugged.

"You need to get out more." Conrad chuckled. He remembered it was the most frustrating part of moving to Spicetown. He had carried that disadvantage around for several months. It had felt as if Spicetown had a secret society that everyone in town was a member of, except him. George 'Bing' Bingham had been mayor when he was hired, and Bing had dragged him around town endlessly introducing him to everyone. Although he had found that tedious, it had been priceless.

"I'm trying." Gwen widened her eyes and leaned forward. "Really, I am."

"I know. It'll come in time. What did they look like?"

"One was a young man. I'd guess early thirties, dark brown hair, about five foot ten, 180 pounds. The other was much older, gray hair, small build, maybe five foot eight, about 140 pounds. The older guy had a sun weathered face and rounded shoulders with a raspy voice. I had trouble understanding him a little. Anyway, these two guys were eating at the table behind me and they were talking about the Emery farm. It sounded like they both worked there."

"I don't know all the guys out there. Some of them are from neighboring towns, but the older one sounds like the farm manager. What did they say?"

"The young guy was whining about losing his job and the old guy told him not to worry. He said Emery's wife was going to keep the farm running just like it had been. Next season, they could do things right and the old lady wouldn't ever bother them. She didn't know anything about the business, and she wouldn't argue with him."

"To some degree," Conrad said. "That's probably true. Arlene wouldn't know much about it and she'd count on the farm manager to keep it going."

"Then the young guy asked if he could get a raise and the older man said that it was long overdue. He planned to see about raising everyone's salary. He didn't think the wife needed the money. He seemed to believe that Hobart Emery had hoarded large amounts of money and that his wife is wealthy now."

"That's not the impression I've gotten, but I don't think Arlene even knows where she's at yet. She seemed very uncertain when I've talked with her, but the mayor has been trying help her. I need to check and see if she's found out anything more."

"The young guy made a comment about not knowing what really killed Mr. Emery and the older man laughed. He said nobody really knows for sure, but it sounded like he went fishing." Gwen tilted her head and smirked. "Only this time the fish won."

"Crass. I guess Hobart wasn't popular with his employees."

"There were other comments that I didn't catch completely. The old guy mentioned changing the planting, something about the boss being afraid to change with the times."

"Hobart did make a change with a small portion of his land this season. He was trying something new." Conrad waved when he saw Sam Snell in his doorway. "Come on in. You remember Officer Kimball?"

"I do. Good to see you." Detective Snell smiled at Gwen as she popped up from her seat and moved to the side of the room.

"I'll write it up for you, Chief." Gwen began inching toward the doorway.

"Have a seat, Sam." Conrad held up his finger and looked at Gwen. "Wait, just a second."

"Yeah?" Officer Kimball leaned on the doorway behind Detective Snell.

"Write up what you heard as much as you can remember, but what was your general take on the situation? I mean, what did you think about the farm situation based on what you heard? You know, your gut reaction."

"The old guy hated Mr. Emery. He thought he was stupid and miserly. He thinks he's got it made now because he's in control of everything."

"Got it," Conrad said with a curt nod of his head to dismiss Officer Kimball. That was exactly the impression Conrad had of Ted Aldridge and that kind of bravado can make a man do a lot of things.

"Sorry to interrupt," Sam Snell said as he placed his travel mug on Conrad's desk and opened a leather binder.

"Not a problem. We were just chatting about a conversation she heard last night. The workers out on Hobart Emery's farm seem pretty happy to have him gone."

"Really? Enough to kill him?"

"It's possible." Conrad raised an eyebrow. "What do you have on the agenda today?"

"I stopped by the nursing home early this morning and talked to Hobart Emery's sister, Beulah. The staff told me she was most alert in the mornings, but they couldn't guarantee her mental state. She wasn't any help, but she wouldn't make a witness anyway. I learned more by talking to the staff. The usual nurse that has the day shift for that hall seemed to know Hobart pretty well. She said he was there almost daily, and he was paying his sister's bills. Naturally, the nursing home is wanting to know who is taking over the care of his sister now."

"Another reason I need to visit his wife again. I've talked to her a couple of times, but she has never seemed to know much. I think she has a couple of friends that have both lost husbands, and they are going to sit down with her to try and sort things out."

"She didn't know anything when I talked to her either." Sam shrugged. "My main mission today is to interview Jeff Wiggins. I'd like to bring him into your office if that's okay."

"Sure."

"I ran some background information on him, and he has a prior conviction of aggravated assault. He did twelve months in state prison for it, but he was young. It was almost twenty years ago. No other arrests or charges."

"That was before my time. He's always worked at the quarry since I've been in town. He's never caused any trouble. I have heard he had a messy divorce that the town's folk like to talk about. Other than that, I never hear about him."

"The divorce is final, but the file is about six inches thick. I didn't have time to read through it, but I did order a copy. From what I gathered, he didn't fair too well."

"That's what the town gossip indicated." Conrad nodded. "Any idea when you might get something on the prints?"

"This afternoon. They told me they'd give it priority."

"You might want to talk to Rick Manning," Conrad said as he warmed his coffee. "He's involved in the quarry and in some of Hobart's financial arrangements. Arlene's explanation didn't make sense to me, but Hobart didn't really tell her what she needs to know. She's forced to depend on what she hears from Rick Manning and he's just an insurance salesman. If you're looking for a financial motive, he might be wrapped up in it somehow. He's Jeff Wiggins' ex-brother in law."

"Good to know. Let's go pick up Mr. Wiggins and see what he has to say."

§

"Hello, Saucy," Cora Mae said when Harvey Salzman appeared at Amanda's office door. "What are you up to today?"

Saucy was still bundled in his coat and the tip of his nose was red from the cold. "Good morning, Mayor. Miss Morgan." Saucy smiled and nodded to Amanda. "I'm just taking my morning walk and thought I'd stop in and say good morning."

"Is everything going well with you?" Cora Mae winked at Amanda. She had shared the news of the yard sign thief with Amanda earlier and had expected Saucy to come by with an update. Cora Mae predicted Saucy couldn't stay angry at a young girl asking for his forgiveness.

"Yes, I think so. The weather is cool, but clear today. I was a bit disheartened to see Hobart Emery won the election when he will not be with us to serve, but I'm glad he did get the votes."

"Yes. I think it will be a comfort to Arlene and you're right, Saucy. It is a horrible shame."

"I think I need to take an extra lap around the block today. The radio said the weather is not going to be so friendly tomorrow and I may not be able to walk."

"Is everything going well on Dill Seed Drive?"

"Oh, yes! We have all received a visit from the young lady who stole our yard signs. I guess the

Chief gave her a good talking to. She was mighty sorry by the time she got to my house."

"Kelly Vaughn?"

"Yes, ma'am. Turns out I knew her grandfather, Ralph Morris! He lived out on Clover Road and I met him when we were young. He was stuck in the snow and I helped him dig out his truck one day. We were good buddies after that. He's been gone a long time now and I lost track of his kids. I had no idea he still had family around here."

"Well, it's nice to see that something good has come from that craziness. I guess you aren't pressing charges?"

"No, I don't plan to do that, but I can't speak for all of Dill Seed Drive. She's still got several more people to visit and a few more on Sage Street. I hope she's learned a lesson from this."

"That would be another positive outcome." Cora pointed at Saucy. "Sometimes, it almost seems that bad things happen only to provide opportunity for something good to come about. Have you ever noticed that?"

'No, ma'am," Harvey said with wide eyes. "That's really deep. I'll have to think on that for a bit."

"Well, you do that, and you make sure you bundle up when you're out walking around. That colder air is moving into the area later today and you don't want to be caught out in it without a hat."

"I'm headed home right now and going to have a cup of hot chocolate. You ladies have a wonderful day."

Saucy waved goodbye over his shoulder as he walked across the City Hall lobby floor and Amanda giggled. "You were right. He caved."

"Saucy has a soft heart."

CHAPTER TWENTY-THREE

"Cora, I'm so glad you invited me to lunch. It's exactly what I needed. I was tired of sitting at home and I needed a reason to get out of the house." Arlene Emery pulled a chair out from the table across from Cora in the Caraway Cafe.

"I invited Peggy Cochran to join us. She's got help in the store today and she said she would come down for lunch if she could. Fall is really when her business picks up."

"Cooler temperatures make you want to knit and quilt." Arlene smiled. "I know Peggy sews all year around, but I'm not very good at sewing clothing. I can do the simple alterations, but to make a whole pattern from scratch is not a relaxing hobby to me. I prefer to quilt, and I do some knitting in the cold months."

"I used to crochet a bit," Cora said. "Oh, here she is."

Peggy Cochran waved at Dorothy Parish when she came in the door to let her know she was joining Cora's table. Slipping off her coat, she pulled out a chair and fell into it. "I made it!"

Peggy blew air from her pursed lips. "I saw a break and I took it. Have you ordered yet?"

"Not yet, but I see Dot heading our way." Cora smiled.

"Ladies! What a wonderful table filled with all my favorite people! What can I get you today?" Dorothy leaned down and hugged Arlene. "I was happy to see Hobart beat Larry Langley."

"Thank you, Dot." Arlene's eyes watered but she smiled.

"Put me down for the special, Dot, and I'd like tea with that." Cora stacked her handbag on top of the coats piled in the empty chair while the other ladies ordered, quickly checking her phone for an update from Conrad. She knew he was going to the quarry today and she was anxious to hear if that questioning revealed anything new.

"Arlene," Cora Mae said after Dot left the table. "Peggy and I want to make sure you know that we are here for you. We've both lost husbands. We've both had to find our own way in the world and recover from that loss. We want to help you navigate through this change. We learned a lot when we went through it and I think we can save you a lot of heartache."

"Oh, Cora, that is so sweet. I can't tell you how much I appreciate the two of you. You've both already helped me so much." Arlene looked around the restaurant. "I know I'm going to need to learn to do things alone, to live alone, to make decisions for myself. It really does help to know you are both there for me."

Peggy leaned forward and lowered her voice. "It's more than just the day to day, Arlene. You have to make business decisions and have some long-range goals. As stuffy as all that sounds, you need some hard facts, some practical plans, and a few people you can trust. Women like us are targets. There are a lot of unscrupulous people in this world that will try to take advantage of you. I know. It happened to me and I'm not going to let it happen to you."

Arlene squeezed Peggy's hand.

"We need to ask some tough questions and we want to help you make some plans for the future if you'll let us." Cora leaned back when a waitress placed a small pot of hot water on the table for her tea.

"Of course. You can ask me anything." Arlene looked at Cora and shrugged. "I may not know the answer, but I'll tell you if I do."

Cora reached in her handbag and pulled out a folder. She and Peggy had talked on the phone that morning to create a list of things that Arlene would need. "There are several different areas where you will need to educate yourself. When you share responsibilities with a partner, you each know things and handle things that the other doesn't get involved in. That leaves you knowing half the story. We need to identify what parts are missing and fill them in. Does that make sense?"

"Perfectly!" Arlene placed her palms together. "That's a wonderful idea."

"Take a look at the lists. You can take them home and see what you can fill in. We can meet again to follow-up on what's missing." Cora handed the folder to Arlene and she flipped it open.

"Oh, I do know some of these," Arlene said as Cora and Peggy looked at each other. "I know where the titles are to the truck and car. I really need to sell the truck and the boat."

Peggy nodded. "Are you on the deeds for the house and the farm?"

"I think so." Arlene frowned. "It's been years since we bought those properties, so I need to make certain."

"Have you talked to Rick Manning about your annuity or whatever it is that he has?" Cora tilted her head.

"I have. He's bringing me copies of everything and said he'd sit down and explain it all." Arlene nodded. "I don't know all of that yet, but I will."

"What about the farm?" Peggy folded her napkin and placed it in her lap. "Is it still running okay? Do you know what's going on there?"

"I don't, but Ted is coming for dinner tonight. Ted Aldridge. That's the man Hobart hired to run the farm. He's going to explain everything that's going on out there and what I need to do. I was going to put the land up for sale or lease after the harvest is done, but Ted says I don't need to do that. He can keep things running just like they are, and I can have a good income from it. I'll have to wait and see what he has to say." Arlene scooted her chair up when the waitress brought over their lunch platters. "By the end of the week, I'm sure I'll have all the answers."

§

"Did I miss anything?" Conrad walked over to the one-way mirrored window and peered in at Detective Snell and Jeff Wiggins inside the interview room.

Officer Gwen Kimball shook her head. "No progress, Chief. I think this is a dead end."

"Jeff was seen on the lake road that morning."

" Yeah, but he doesn't have anything else. No leverage." Gwen shook her head again. "Maybe he could have waited for the prints to come back. If he gets a match, he'll have to do this all over again."

Conrad couldn't argue with that. He didn't follow Sam Snell's logic either, but it was different when you had multiple cases to work. He remembered those days and you couldn't always do things at the best time. You had to do them when you could find time. "I'm hoping the detective will want to go out to the farm. I'd like to get more information out there. I didn't have much luck the first time I went."

"Does this Wiggins guy have a sheet?" Kimball frowned and wrinkled her nose. "He sounds like someone who has been in prison before."

"Yeah, but he just did a year, and it was a long time ago." Conrad pointed at the window. "He does have some tattoos on his hands."

"He keeps talking about an ex-wife. It sounds like Hobart Emery helped him out when his wife was taking all his money, but he doesn't talk like he appreciated Hobart at all."

"I don't think he'd be the owner operator of the Spicetown Rock Quarry today if Hobart hadn't taken him under his wing. On the surface, Hobart's endeavors always seem very altruistic, yet the people involved always seem bitter about him. I can't figure it out."

Gwen looked over at Conrad. "He helped them out the way he thought they needed help. He didn't give them what they wanted."

Conrad frowned. "Beggars can't be choosers."

"Well, sometimes other people think they know what's best for you and they force it on you when you don't want it. Does that make sense?"

Conrad nodded.

"I don't think Jeff Wiggins wanted to run the rock quarry and I think he's miserable. It's just the way he talks about it to the detective that makes me think he'd be gone in a minute if he could find an easy way to make money. He's not a hard worker at heart. He wants something for nothing."

"If that's true, I'm surprised he didn't kill Hobart earlier. When they worked together, his wife told me that there was a life insurance policy payable to Jeff. As far as I know, he doesn't gain anything for Hobart's death now."

"Do we have the business records? Maybe there's debt in Hobart's name that would get cleared if he died."

"We'll have to ask Sam that."

"Do we even know if this guy fishes?" Gwen turned around and looked at Conrad. "I haven't heard the detective ask him why he was down at Eagle Bay Road Friday morning. Shouldn't he have been at work?"

Conrad chuckled. "Maybe you need to be in there instead of Snell."

"Maybe." Gwen smirked.

CHAPTER TWENTY-FOUR

"Cora, I'm worried."

"Arlene?" Cora Mae sat up and pressed the phone to her ear. "What's the matter? Has something happened?"

"Rick Manning just left my house. He called me this morning to say he was bringing the copies of the policies that Hobart purchased from him like he promised. He got very defensive and short with me on the phone though. I wasn't accusing him of anything. I even offered to come down and pick them up to pay for the copies."

"Arlene, he should have expected you to ask for copies. It's perfectly normal. People lose their policies all the time."

"Well, I have copies now. He just left. He knocked on my door, handed me a huge stack of paper and said he was in a rush. He didn't even come inside. I don't know what all this paperwork means, but some of it has the quarry listed and even Jeff's name. I'm not sure what I have here."

"Well," Cora Mae said twirling sideways in her office chair. "I could come look at it, but I'm no expert. Maybe that's what we need."

"I'm hesitant to contact Rick and ask questions now. He seemed so irritated by my request, but if he's in charge of these policies, I have to deal with him somehow."

"Let's see what we can find out. Charlie Elkins handled my policies when Bing died, and he's been in the insurance business for many years. Let me call him and see if he's willing to take a look. He might be able to save you a lot of time and worry."

"Do you think he would do that? I could bring them to town--"

"Let me call him and ask. If he has time tomorrow to look over them, I'll pick them up on my way home tonight. I can drop them by his office in the morning on my way to work. You don't need to make a special trip out."

"Thank you, Cora. I knew you would know just what to do."

§

"Chief." Detective Snell appeared at Conrad's door just as he turned from gazing out the window. "Got a minute?"

"Sure. Come on in. I was just thinking about who else knew where Hobart was that Friday morning."

Sam Snell took the seat across from Conrad. "Wiggins claims he didn't. He can't explain what he was doing driving down Eagle Bay Road Friday morning, but he says he didn't know Hobart was there."

"Wiggins can't tell you why he was there?"

"Nope. He says he was just out driving around without any real destination in mind." Detective Snell smirked.

"He doesn't live anywhere near the lake and I'm assuming he was expected at the quarry. When you run a business alone, you almost live there from what I can tell from others."

"Yeah, I need to ask him who was running the show at the quarry while he was joy riding."

"What do you plan to do with him? Do you have a statement?" Conrad leaned back and stretched.

"That's why I'm here. I'd like to hold him until we can check out his story. I can have him transported to the county jail if he's in your way."

"No. No, he can stay here in holding. That's not a problem at all."

"I appreciate it. Then I can check on some things and talk to him again tomorrow. I'm hoping to hear from the lab any minute on those prints. If the prints on the oar match the ones on the coffee mug your mayor gave us, the prosecutor's office will probably want to file charges. If all that happens, I'll have him transported to the county jail."

Conrad nodded. "I'd like to talk to Hazel Linton again. She knows what goes on around Eagle Bay Road. She may be able to tell me exactly what Jeff Wiggins was doing out there."

"Really? What are you thinking?"

Conrad smiled. "I'm thinking Jeff's a young single man and he could be driving out there to check on someone completely unrelated to Hobart Emery. If he's going out there frequently, Hazel will know. She may not know who he's visiting or watching, but it might be that he has a lady friend out there."

"Why wouldn't he just tell me that?"

Conrad raised one eyebrow and tilted his head. Detective Snell must not have much imagination. "Mr. Wiggins may be involved in something he doesn't want public."

"Oh, you mean he might have been driving by to see if the husband was home?" Sam Snell nodded.

"Or maybe his ex-wife lives down there and he's checking on her. I don't know. It's just a speculation on my part, but I can see him not wanting to tell that story unless he thinks he has to. After a night in holding, he may tell you more, but I just thought it couldn't hurt to see what Hazel knows."

"Yeah, please call her. See if she can add anything that can help."

"The other issue I was thinking about," Conrad said as he pushed away from his desk. "Ted Aldridge told me that he knew Hobart was headed to the lake. I don't know if he told anyone else on the farm. I've got a list of Hobart's employees here. They still need to be checked out."

Sam frowned and accepted the list that Conrad offered him. "This is going to take some time."

"I can have my guys run the basic background on each of them, if that will help."

"Yeah, it would. I'd really appreciate it if they could do that."

"Sure." Conrad scratched his head. "I'd like to go back out to the farm and touch base with Aldridge again now that we know a little bit more."

"I have no problem with that, Chief. Feel free to interview anyone that can help us. You know the folks here better than I do and I trust your judgment."

"I appreciate that."

"For now, I'm going to head back to the Sheriff's office and do some paperwork, but I'll be back tomorrow. Can you take care of Wiggins for me?"

"Sure thing," Conrad said as he stood. "I'll see that he gets our best room."

Detective Snell chuckled as he walked down the hallway.

§

"Amanda, I'm going to shut my door for about ten minutes. I need to make some phone calls."

"Okay. I'll try to stop everybody from barging in, but we've had more people through here this week than we usually have in a month!"

"Everyone wants to talk about the election." Cora grabbed her head with both hands. "It's driving me crazy. That's going to be one of my phone calls. The Spicetown Star needs to print something to answer these questions. I can't be 4-1-1 for the whole town all day. I can't get anything else done."

"That's the one person that hasn't been in to visit, the Spicetown Star. I'm surprised they aren't at least calling to ask questions."

"I'm about to give them some answers before they ask! Have you seen Larry Langley come in City Hall today? I thought he might stop in. I really wish he would make an appearance. That would answer a lot of questions that people have. He needs to stop hiding and let them know he is still their councilman until the end of the calendar year."

"I haven't seen him." Amanda shrugged. "He's probably feeling a little self-conscious."

"I thought he'd be down here trying to talk to his fellow council members, hoping they would nominate him for the vacancy."

"Do you think they'll do that?" Amanda frowned. "Doesn't the vote tell them that Larry isn't what the people want?"

"It was a bit of a landslide," Cora whispered. "I'm not certain the council cares. They can pick whoever they want, and they want someone who will agree with them."

"Oh." Amanda scrunched up her nose. "I guess it's better to work with the devil you know than the devil you don't. It's something my mother always says."

Cora Mae chuckled. "They have had years of experience with Larry. They also have to run for election themselves, so we'll see. It will be interesting to see who they pick." Cora waved her hand when Amanda's desk phone rang to indicate she should answer and ducked into her office to shut the door. It seemed no one knew what to think about the election results and that needed to be addressed.

Cora flipped through sticky notes on her computer monitor and desk light until she found the number for The Spicetown Star and asked to speak with Paulie Childers. The staff at the local newspaper was small, but Paulie had been promoted recently and assigned to handle the city events and crime topics.

"Mayor! How can I help you?"

Cora smiled at the sound of shock in Paulie's voice. He was usually seeking her out, not the other way around. "Paulie, we have a problem and I'm hoping you can fix it."

"I am happy to help any way that I can. What's our problem?"

"Paulie, I'm getting calls, texts and visits constantly. The people of this town need to know what the election laws say. They don't realize that Larry is still their councilman and they don't know what the election results mean. Are you working on an article that will explain all this? Have you talked to Ned Carey about it? You did such a wonderful job the day before the election by explaining the ballots to everyone. Now that we have the results, we need your expertise again."

"Uh, no ma'am. I haven't done that. I've been busy working with the Sheriff's office on the developments with Hobart Emery's case. They've been really helpful, and I'm working on a story that will keep everyone up to date on the status of that investigation."

"Hm, well. Paulie, has anyone asked you what is going on with the Emery case? I mean, are people stopping you, calling you, just to find out where the police are on that investigation?"

"Well, no but--"

"Do you know why that is, Paulie? Let me tell you why that is. They aren't asking about Hobart's case because they're consumed with what in the world is going to happen next since the winner of the election is dead! They want to know if Larry is going to win by default. Is there going to be another election? Is his wife going to take the position? Is the town just going to be short one councilman? You see, there are a number of possibilities and I've been asked about them all."

"Yes, ma'am. I can see where they might think that."

"But you know what, Paulie? There are election laws and they're really obscure. Most people never have any reason to know them. It doesn't need to be a really big article. They just need the basic questions answered and I'm sure Ned Carey will give you all the quotes you need." Paulie Childers loved quotes.

"That's a really good idea, Mayor. I appreciate the tip."

"Well, I would really appreciate you getting that much needed information out in front of every citizen, so we are all on the same page. No pun intended." Cora Mae chuckled.

"Will do, Mayor. I'm sure I can work that in."

"Thank you, Paulie. You have a good day." Cora hung up the phone and rested her head in her hands. Paulie had lost touch with his audience, and his own fame was crowding his judgment since he had been promoted. She sighed as she looked at the clock. It was probably too late to expect it in tomorrow's paper, so she would have to endure another day of questions.

Now to call Charlie Elkins! Cora pulled open her desk drawer and rummaged around in her purse. She knew she had a business card in there somewhere, and after several attempts, she found the Elkins Insurance Agency. Charlie was an odd bird. In fact, Bing had secretly called him Charlie Peacock in jest. Charlie was a tall, thin, delicate man who dressed exquisitely. He was poised and almost dainty in his movements, but his head did strut slightly ahead of his body when he walked, giving him that bird-like appearance. All kidding aside, Bing had always felt confident in the advice

Charlie had given him and Cora continued to use him for all her insurance needs.

"Good afternoon, Charlie. This is Cora Mae Bingham calling. How are you today?"

"Madame Mayor! How delightful to hear from you. My day has suddenly improved."

Cora Mae blushed. Charlie's grandiose style was always flattering. "I'm so glad. I'm calling to see if you might have a little time tomorrow for a small favor. I have a friend who has some policies that her late husband purchased, and she can't make heads or tails of them."

"They can be disturbingly difficult to comprehend. It's a shame, really."

"Yes, well. I wondered if you might have time tomorrow to take a peek at them. Maybe you can let her know if she's in a good place or not. She could really use some guidance she can trust."

"I am at your disposal."

"If it's okay, I'll run them by your office in the morning and leave them with you."

"A wonderful plan! I will see you tomorrow morning."

CHAPTER TWENTY-FIVE

"Hello, Ted." Arlene Emery held the screen door open and waved Ted Aldridge through the door. "I'm glad you're here. Please come on into the kitchen. I've still got a few things to do and we can talk while I finish up if you don't mind."

"Not at all, ma'am. I appreciate the offer of a home cooked meal. I don't get one of those too often. I just wish I could have run home first to clean up. I feel bad bringing in the farm dust."

"Oh, don't be silly. You are just fine. Never be ashamed of a hard day at work." Arlene tapped the kitchen table as she walked by. "Have a seat. I've got a few things still in the oven and I need to mash the potatoes."

"Everything smells so good. I usually grab something quick in town when I get off work. I live a good drive away and I'm always too hungry to wait until I get home in the evening."

"Eating out can be a nice treat, but I don't think I'd want to do it every day. I didn't realize you had a long drive. Do you have a place out in the county?"

"No, I've been staying at my brother's place in Milford. I've been looking for something closer."

"Milford! That's an hour's drive, isn't it?" Arlene rinsed out her mixing bowl and left it in the sink.

"Almost." Ted shrugged. "Sometimes it seems like I just got home and it's time to drive back."

"I can imagine" Arlene drained her potatoes. "I'm sure we can find you something in town that will save you a lot of driving."

"Mr. Emery had talked to me about putting a trailer out at the farm. That way I'd be handy for the early morning deliveries. He talked with Mrs. Landry about her lots, but I don't guess anything came of that."

Arlene frowned. "I think I hear someone in the driveway."

When the dog began to bark, Ted stood up. "Let me go check."

Arlene rinsed off her spoon and dried her hands on a kitchen towel. Glancing at the clock, she expected it to be Cora Mae coming by for the policies.

When Arlene reached the living room, she saw that Ted had opened the door for Cora. "Evening," Ted nodded his head. "I'll just go get Mrs. Emery."

"I'm right here. Come on in, Cora Mae. Let me get that envelope for you. Do you two know each other?"

Ted shook his head.

"Cora, this is Ted Aldridge. He takes care of the farm. Ted, this is Cora Bingham. She's the Mayor of Spicetown."

"Oh! Glad to meet you, ma'am, uh, Mayor." Ted held out his hand and Cora shook it.

"It's nice to meet you, too. I don't believe we've met before."

"No, ma'am. I don't get into town much."

"I see." Cora smiled and searched for Arlene who had disappeared into the back bedroom. Ted was nervous and his eyes darted around the living room. "I'm sorry if I interrupted dinner."

"Oh, no. I just got here, and Mrs. Emery was working in the kitchen. We were just in there talking when you drove up."

"Cora." Arlene walked into the room waving a Manila envelope that was at least an inch thick. "I'm sorry to keep you waiting. It wasn't where I thought I put it." Arlene rolled her eyes. "I don't have my head on straight nowadays."

Cora reached out for the envelope. "I'll run it by in the morning and you should hear something later in the day." Cora reached for the screen door. She didn't want to talk in front of Ted, but she gave Arlene a questioning look and glanced at Ted. "We'll talk tomorrow. I'll let you two get back to dinner."

"Call me when you can." Arlene waved as Cora walked to her car and then turned back to the kitchen door. "I hope my potatoes aren't getting cold."

§

"Chief." Officer Harold Hobson, who everyone called Wink because he had one eye that didn't open all the way, nodded a salute as he walked by Conrad's office door. He was starting his evening shift and Conrad was ready to go home.

"Hey, Wink. Jeff Wiggins is in holding. Snell interviewed him today, but he wanted him held overnight. If there are any problems with him, you can call the Sheriff's Office."

"Okay, Chief. Any progress?"

"Not by my measure." Conrad slipped his arm into his coat. "But I'm just an observer."

Wink chuckled. "Frustrating, isn't it?"

"A little." Conrad nodded. "But tomorrow is another day."

Conrad reached for Briscoe's leash and saw Dean Teggers walk into the lobby of the police department on the front door video monitor in the dispatcher's cubicle. "Ready for dinner?" Briscoe crawled out from under the desk in the dispatch cubicle and stretched his back. Rubbing Briscoe's ear, Conrad clipped the leash on to his harness.

"Chief?" Dean Teggers extended his hand. "I'm Dean Teggers. I don't know if you remember me or not--"

"Sure, I do. How are you, Mr. Teggers?" Conrad shook his hand.

"I'm good. I'm sorry it's so late, but I got held up a little at work today. I wanted to see what I needed to do to file a complaint against that young lady who tampered with my yard signs. She came by and talked with me, but unlike my neighbors, she didn't change my mind one bit. What she did was wrong, and she needs to learn a lesson from it. I'd like to press charges."

"All right. That's certainly your prerogative. Officer Crawford will get your basic information and take care of that for you." Conrad glanced at Officer Crawford. "This is a trespass and property theft charge."

"I got it, Chief." Officer Crawford pulled a clipboard off a wall hook and slid some paperwork under the clip.

"We're off to get some dinner. Goodnight." Conrad waved before turning to walk down the hallway. Briscoe's nails clicked on the linoleum flooring. When Conrad felt his cell phone buzz in his chest pocket, he decided he was too tired to answer and walked out the side door to his car.

§

Frank Parrish held up his hand for silence. The Spicetown Merchants Association had secured a meeting room in the town library for the evening's meeting; however, they had been asked to keep the noise down to a polite level. He had doubted his wife's ability to do that, but the meeting room was a comfortable spot for their gathering. "Remember, guys. No shouting."

"Where's the boss?" Ned Carey chuckled when he saw Frank's smirk.

"My wife is making some copies for everyone. She'll be right back."

"Dot told me to get here early, but I'm not sure why." Ned looked around the room and waved to his buddy, Ted Parrish, as he walked in the door. Ted was Frank's brother and he owned Chervil Drugstore

Dot returned with a stack of papers in her hand and began passing them out to each person seated in the room.

"Dot, are you sure you have enough chairs? Do you want me to go get some more?" Ted hung his coat near the door.

"We have more back in the corner." Dorothy pointed behind the door. "We won't need as many chairs tonight. I think a couple of our members have been arrested since our last meeting, so I thought I better invite the attorney to this one." Dorothy nodded her head toward Ned Carey and laughed at his shocked expression.

"Now wait a minute," Ned said, holding up a finger. "I thought this merchant representation stuff was all partnerships and such. I try to stay away from criminal law."

"Do we have Spicetown retailers that are criminals?" Levi Nauchtman, owner of the Nutmeg Bed & Breakfast, called out.

"Larry Langley is out of jail, isn't he?" Brian Stotlar, Amanda Morgan's beau and owner of Stotlar's Plant Nursery, asked of those sitting around him. He was certain Amanda had told him of Larry's release, but that didn't mean he hadn't been arrested again.

"Yes, Larry is out of jail, but that young girl from Paxton-- Kelly. She was at our last meeting and I heard the Chief yanked her right out of the bakery one morning and took her to jail. I guess we won't be getting a Burger Buddy after all." Wesley Parker, the owner of the Wasabi Women Dance Club, shrugged his shoulders. "And I heard her husband was going to build it out by my place. I was looking forward to it."

"Jeff Wiggins is in jail tonight." Rick Manning made the announcement and looked around the room. "I'm not sure why. Does anyone know anything about it?"

"Okay, everybody. Let's get started. We aren't here to gossip." Dorothy Parrish stood up in front of the lectern and the room fell silent. "At the last meeting we discussed several different ideas that we may want to explore. The list I handed out is a cost estimate for each item. We will have to prioritize which of the items we each need the most. I invited our City Attorney Ned Carey tonight so that he can give you an overview of what he can offer the association in the legal department. This way you will have the information you need to determine how this item should be ranked in our listing and to give everyone an opportunity to ask some questions. Ned."

Dorothy stepped aside from the lectern and waved Ned to the front.

"Evening, folks." Ned nodded to the audience. "Dot and I chatted about this a bit, but I can't predict just what might come up for everyone. I can help you with incorporation paperwork and I can offer a free consult on other issues, but if you need personal injury or insurance litigation, I'll only be able to offer you a referral to another attorney."

"And if I get arrested?" Ted Parrish called out.

"You're on your own, Ted." Ned's round belly shook as he laughed, and Frank popped up from his chair to quiet the group's laughter with hand gestures.

Levi Nauchtman raised his hand and Ned pointed at him. "When you say referrals, do you mean you know attorneys who specialize in different areas, and you would get us in to see them?"

"Yes." Ned Carey nodded. "I have worked with several attorneys in Paxton on slip and fall cases with the city as well as other firms that handle insurance settlements. I can recommend someone to you based on your need."

"Do you know why Jeff Wiggins is in jail tonight?" Rick Manning asked Ned, but then turned around in his seat. "Does anybody know?"

Ned looked over at Dorothy and frowned. Dorothy stepped up to the lectern as Ned walked away. "Rick, I don't think anyone knows anything at all about Jeff. I'm not sure why you think we would, but it's not--."

"Somebody has to know. I mean I called the police department, and they won't talk to me. They told me to call the Sheriff's Office. I called them and they said to call back tomorrow. This is--"

"How do you know that Jeff Wiggins was arrested today?" Dorothy pointed at Rick.

"My sister told me. Someone that works at the quarry called and told her that the police came today to arrest him. They just took him away and no one can get any information."

"You seem very upset about it, Rick." Dorothy squinted her eyes. "I wish we could help you, but I'm sure you will be able to find out tomorrow morning." The room was silent for several seconds and then Dorothy announced they would move to the next agenda item. Before the meeting ended, Rick Manning slipped out the back door.

CHAPTER TWENTY-SIX

"Good morning?" Conrad stood with one hand on his hip and the other holding Briscoe's leash. He had just walked into the police station and found Cora Mae standing at his copy machine feeding paper into the tray. "Is your copier down?"

"Oh, no. I just came by to copy these documents for you before I take them to Charlie."

"Documents? Charlie?"

"Did I not tell you?" Cora Mae twisted her head to one side. "I guess I haven't seen you. Oh well, these documents are the insurance policies from Rick Manning. Arlene got them and I'm taking them over to Charlie Elkins. He's going to take a look and give Arlene the lowdown on what she's got here. She tried to talk to Rick and he got a little short with her. She's concerned that things aren't as they were first presented."

"Hmm." Conrad unclipped Briscoe's leash so he could jog over to Georgia Marks in dispatch. "Funny you should mention Rick Manning. He was at the Merchants meeting last night and Ned

Carey tells me that he was acting strange. He was upset that Wiggins was detained yesterday."

"Jeff Wiggins is in jail?" Cora tilted her head to the other side. "We need to catch up."

"We do." Conrad chuckled. "I don't know what today will hold. Detective Snell is coming back over. I'm hoping we go out to the farm to interview, but so far, he keeps going in other directions."

"I met the farm manager last night, Ted Aldridge." Cora raised one eyebrow and grinned.

"You did? Where did you meet him? You didn't go to the farm, did you?"

"He was at Arlene's house last night when I went to pick up these policies."

"What was he doing there?"

"I plan to ask that question today. I can tell you what it looked like. It looked like they were playing house, but all I was told was that they were preparing dinner."

"Oh, really. That's interesting. Preparing dinner."

"Yep." Cora smiled. "If you do get out to the farm today, you might want to ask him how his dinner went."

"I might do that."

"And I'll see what the other side has to say." Cora banged the edges of the paper on the table to straighten the stack before handing them to Conrad. "I've got to run now. I'll talk to you later."

§

"Good morning, Arlene." Cora reached for her mouse as she cradled her cell phone with the other hand and clicked open her email application. She was getting a late start today.

"Morning, Cora."

"I just wanted to let you know that I dropped off your policies with Charlie Elkins this morning. I also gave him your phone number and he's going to give you a call once he takes a look at everything. I don't know if he'll want you to come down to his office or not, but if you need me, just let me know. I'm happy to go with you if you'd like."

"Thank you so much. You have been such a blessing to me. I do appreciate your help with this. I don't understand what got into Rick Manning. He was so accommodating the first time we talked and then when I asked him why there were several policies, he became agitated. Maybe I just called at a bad time, but those papers didn't look like what he described to me. I'm a little worried."

"I'm hoping Charlie can explain it clearly and there won't be need for worry. How did your dinner go last night?"

"Oh, with Ted? That has me a bit confused, too. He told me over the phone that he knew exactly how to run the farm and could just continue Hobart's work there without any change. I asked him several questions last night and I'm concerned with the answers I got. I need to go out there and clean out Hobart's office. Most of his paperwork is at home, but he did keep a small office out there. I think Ted assumes that I don't know anything at all. That's just not true. Hobart talked about the farm all the time. I know all about his plans to test out the edamame and slowly transition the farm."

"Ted may be worried that he'll lose his job unless he convinces you that you need him."

"I just don't know, Cora. I think it could be profitable, but I don't know if I can manage it on my own."

"Why haven't I ever seen him before? Does he not live around here?" Not too many people could live or work in Spicetown and escape Cora's observation, yet she'd never met Ted Aldridge.

"He told me he is living in Milford right now, but it sounded temporary. I don't really know where he's from or where Hobart found him. He's worked out there for several years."

"I'm happy to ride out there with you whenever you need to go. We can go out and clean the office this afternoon if you'd like. I don't have any meetings scheduled today and it gets dark so early now."

"That would make me feel so much better. I'll call you once I hear from Charlie."

"I'll be here. Now, don't you worry yourself all day about this. We'll figure it out." Cora hung up the phone looking forward to this field trip.

§

Detective Snell accepted a cup of coffee from Officer Roy Asher and took a seat in Conrad's office.

"The prints don't belong to Wiggins. It was late yesterday before the lab called, but no match. I guess I'll cut him loose today."

"Do you want to take a look at the list of employees from the farm? Officer Tabor has checked on all of them and there might be some that you'll want to talk to." Conrad pulled out his office chair. "I know there are several that have a criminal background. The farm manager can probably tell us if there were any that didn't come to work that Friday morning."

"Yeah. Yeah, we'll get to that, but I have a few names that Wiggins gave me and I want to talk to them first. He had some guys call out from work Friday morning and I need to see if they have an alibi. They were long time employees. Worked for Hobart since the early years and didn't have a nice thing to say about him, according to Wiggins. I want to see if that turns up anything."

"Okay. I have copies of the insurance policies Hobart took out. I just got them this morning, so I haven't read everything yet, but it looks like he had a work policy and a couple of family policies that--"

"Anything out of the ordinary jump out at you?" Detective Snell bounced his foot and took another gulp of coffee.

"The insurance agent is concerning. He was giving the wife the impression he was managing funds, when he's not equipped for that, and then last night, he made a spectacle of himself at a town meeting. He told everyone that Jeff Wiggins was arrested, and no one would tell him why. He seemed overly concerned about it and I can't help but think there is more to it. Rick Manning is Jeff's ex-brother-in-law. That doesn't sound like a close relationship although it might have been once."

"Maybe you need to ask Wiggins about that." Snell pointed his index finger at Conrad. "I can run out to the quarry and you can pull Wiggins out for a little talk before releasing him. See what he has to say about the insurance agent."

Conrad nodded. "If it's anything promising, I'll ask Rick Manning if he'd like to make a statement. It would seem he had a good relationship with both Wiggins and Hobart Emery. Maybe he has something to share."

"Good idea!" Detective Snell tossed his paper coffee cup into the trash can. "I'll check back in with you later."

CHAPTER TWENTY-SEVEN

"I'm sorry to disturb you." Arlene Emery stepped into Amanda Morgan's office. "I was told I could find the mayor in here."

"Yes, she's in."

"I'm sorry. I'm Arlene Emery. I spoke with the mayor earlier."

"Yes. Please come in. I'm Amanda Morgan. Just let me check and see if she's on the phone."

"Thank you, dear." Arlene slipped her arms out of her coat.

"Arlene, come in." Cora called out and Amanda waved Arlene toward the door.

"She's right in here."

"Arlene, come in. Have a seat. I would have come to your house--"

"No. No need to do that. I came into town to meet with Charlie. A very nice man, by the way, and it just made sense for me to stop by. There was no need for you to get out. I just wanted to check in and see if you had time to run out to the farm with me."

"Sure. I'm happy to, but what did Charlie say? Did you get all your questions answered? Is everything going to be okay?"

"It is," Arlene said as she perched on the edge of the chair across from Cora Mae's desk. "It was really complicated, but Charlie explained everything and he's going to take it over for me. He deals with the same company that Hobart bought these policies through, so I'm moving everything over to Charlie. He even called Rick Manning for me and that's all settled."

"And you are going to have the funds you need?"

"I am! In fact, it's better than I imagined. Hobart made a policy for me, one for the quarry and one for Beulah, his sister. When he left the quarry, he changed that policy over to me and rolled all three policies into an insurance trust, which helps with taxes. It was set up so that there was one administrator who would take care of Beulah with her portion and pay my expenses."

"That sounds like a great plan!" Cora held her palms up.

"It could have been except Rick made himself administrator and he's not qualified to do that. Charlie said it was very unethical."

"That might explain why he didn't like you questioning him."

"Yes, but it all turned out for the best. The trust is not three years old yet, so it reverts back to three individual policies. I don't get the tax benefit he intended, but the payments are the same."

"That does sound a little complicated." Cora Mae frowned. "The quarry policy is going to you?"

"Yes. Charlie had to call them and confirm everything, but Hobart changed the beneficiary before he created the trust. If he'd done it the other way around, Jeff Wiggins would have been the beneficiary when the trust dissolved."

"Oh, my." Cora grimaced. Perhaps Rick was unaware of that small nuance.

"Charlie took care of it and I'll get a check next week. He also set up an annuity for me and explained how we can manage Beulah's portion. I'm probably going to need a power of attorney to help Beulah, but there isn't any other family, so Charlie got me an appointment with someone in Paxton that will help me."

"I'm so glad this worked out so well!" Cora clapped her hands together. This was the best possible outcome. "Now, you mentioned you have some concerns about the farm manager."

"Yes. I need to tell you about our dinner."

"You can tell me on the way. Let's run out there."

Arlene nodded and reached for her coat.

"Amanda, can you empty out that copy paper box over there for me?"

"Sure, Mayor."

"We can take a couple of boxes with us so we have something to pack Hobart's files in." Cora jumped up and opened her desk drawer to pull out her handbag. "I have some fabric shopping bags in my car, too. We want to try and get as much as we can with this trip. Is Ted expecting you?"

"No, he's not, and there is a question that's unanswered. Actually, there are a couple of questions. He wants to know if I'm going to continue the farm after this harvest, and he wants to know about the lot. The lot that Hobart bought from Miriam is right across from the office. Ted wants to live there."

"Live there?"

"He said Hobart bought the lot because he intended to put a trailer on it for him." Arlene shrugged.

"Is that true?"

"No. I think Ted is telling me this because he doesn't think I know anything. He talks about the farm the same way. He told me several things last night that I know are not true, but I didn't let on that I knew. I wanted to see how far he would go, and there seems to be no end to his deceit. I was really disappointed in some of the things he said."

"I didn't think Ted and Hobart got along that well." Cora slipped into her coat and grabbed the boxes.

"I'm parked out front." Arlene led the way through Amanda's office, and Cora Mae told Amanda she'd be back soon.

"No, they didn't." Arlene walked slowly down the front steps of City Hall so Cora could catch up. "And Hobart always said that Ted Aldridge couldn't find his behind with both hands. He said he had to tell him every little thing to do because he was lost on his own. They fought constantly."

"So why did Hobart keep him around?" Cora shoved the boxes in the back seat and climbed into Arlene's car.

"The workers liked him. He said they worked well for Ted, but he knew Ted bad-mouthed him all day long. He kept him around because he did follow his orders. He just had to go out there every day and check on things. He couldn't leave things to Ted to get done. That's why I don't think Ted can run things."

"So, you are thinking about letting him go?"

"I have to. Even if I wanted to continue the farm, I can't trust it to him."

"Why did Hobart buy that lot from Miriam?"

"Oh, he was going to put a trailer out there, but it wasn't for Ted. It was for Mickey Barnes. He's a farmhand that Hobart hired with the intention of training him to take over. He didn't even plan to keep Ted next season. I don't think Ted was aware of that."

"Have you talked to this Mickey at all? Was he aware of Hobart's intentions?"

"No. Hobart hadn't made him any promises or told him what he was considering. He wanted to see how he did on his own first. Then if things went well, Hobart was planning to fire Ted and promote Mickey."

"I don't know how you got through that dinner! I don't take well to people trying to manipulate me or take advantage. I'd probably have told him the truth and tossed him on the porch!" Cora Mae giggled. "That wouldn't have been the smart thing to do. I realize the season isn't over and you don't want him to quit on you, but I would have been angry."

"Oh, I was. It just made me more confident that I'm doing the right thing, and I'm looking forward to firing him." Arlene slapped the steering wheel and chuckled. "I would have been nervous about doing that, but he has made it so much easier on me now."

"I remember you telling me that you got along well with Ted even though Hobart didn't."

"That's true," Arlene said as she turned the car into the dirt road that ran to the farm office. "He was always careful to be respectful and kind to me when I was around. I don't come out here often, but some evenings I would be with Hobart when we stopped at the farm on our way to dinner. Ted was always kind to me, and he was last night as well. He just wasn't truthful, and I can't excuse that."

"I understand completely." Cora Mae nodded as Arlene parked her car near the office door.

"I'm sure he will be polite today, too." Arlene opened her car door and turned to Cora. "Thank you so much for coming with me."

Cora patted Arlene's arms and grabbed her handbag. "Let's go."

CHAPTER TWENTY-EIGHT

"Morning, Jeff." Conrad pulled a chair away from the table in the interview room and turned it sideways. Planting one foot in the seat of the chair, he tossed a yellow lined notepad on the table.

"Chief." Jeff's eyes were red and his complexion pale. He did not look well rested.

"Let's see if we can get a statement down and get you released today. Are you ready to do that?"

"Yeah, Chief. What do I need to do?"

"Let's lay some groundwork first. You started working for Hobart years ago. Right? When was that?"

"Almost twenty years ago."

Conrad nodded and pointed at the pad. "Let's start there. Write that down. You started working for Hobart twenty years ago. You got along well back then?"

"Yeah." Jeff nodded. "He was good to me. He said he saw something in me and thought I could do more. He started teaching me the ropes. He pulled me into the office after a few years and started showing me how the business ran. I helped him."

"And he helped you?" Conrad leaned his elbow on his knee and peered at Jeff.

"He did."

"So, when did everything go south?"

Jeff looked down at the table. "Hobart was a really smart businessman and he was a good teacher. As long as he was in training mode, you know, teaching you how things went, he was real supportive. After he thought you were trained though, he was hard to please. He expected me to be as good as he was, and that just wasn't ever going to happen. He was always disappointed in me after that and we argued a lot. He was so negative, and after a while, I started fighting back. I was doing the best I could, but he just wouldn't accept that as good enough. He always found fault."

"But the two of you became partners in the business. Was that before the arguing started?"

"Yeah, but I shouldn't have done it. We had been working together a couple of years by then, and he complained about everything I did. I didn't say a word. I just kept trying harder. I thought I could take it, but after a few years of being beaten down by him, I just went off. After that, things were even worse. I took the partnership because I thought it would pay off better in the long run. That hasn't been the case. I made more money as an employee, but I couldn't undo it. He tricked me."

"So, you felt set up by Hobart? You felt like the partnership deal was just a way to pay you less?" Conrad put his foot down and turned the chair back toward the table.

"Yeah. It saved him money and it freed him up to walk away. It was part of his plan to retire, but he never told me that."

Conrad sat down in the chair and leaned forward on his elbows. "You had to know he was nearing retirement age. You knew about the life insurance policy, too. Didn't you?"

"Yeah. I knew he took out a policy to help me with the business in case he died before he retired. We never talked about what happened to the insurance money after he retired. We just didn't talk about him retiring at all. I guess I should have thought about it, but I was too focused on what changes it made for me at the time."

"How is your relationship with Rick Manning?"

"He's my ex-wife's brother, but we get along okay. He's just looking out for Twyla, and sometimes he is a good mediator for us when we don't want to talk to each other."

"Rick must have gotten along well with Hobart, too. Is that why Rick did the insurance policies for the business or did you recommend him?"

"Hobart already knew Rick. He had used him before."

"Okay." Conrad leaned back in his chair. "So, first you did the partnership agreement and then you did the insurance policy. Right?"

Jeff nodded.

"Did Rick Manning contact you about the insurance policies after Hobart retired? Did he tell you that Hobart had changed the beneficiary on the policy?"

"No." Jeff leaned back in his chair. "Hobart told me."

"Oh, so you were okay with that. You expected it?"

"I was surprised when he told me, but I had forgotten all about the policy by that time. He told me he was doing it because I couldn't buy him out like I was supposed to and at least his wife would have something to show for all the work he did with the quarry. He told me I had let it all go downhill."

"But didn't he draw pension from the quarry?"

"Yeah, but it was from some investment he paid into over the years. I don't have any retirement plan, but he had some fund he paid into so he could draw retirement. I don't really know what it was. Rick could maybe tell you. I think he helped him with that."

"A few years ago Hobart made some changes to his policies and created an insurance trust. Did your brother-in-law tell you about that?"

"Not at the time he didn't, but later he told me about it, after Hobart died."

"And what did he tell you?" Conrad folded his arms over his chest.

"He said it was going to be messy because Hobart died before the trust was done. I didn't understand, but he said it took three years to work and I would get paid on the old policy since he died before the three years were up. I'll never see any money from it though. Rick already told Twyla and she'll get everything. She takes everything I have. I'm sure she'll find a way to get that, too."

"And he told you this after Hobart died? When exactly?"

"He called me." Jeff frowned. "I'd have to look at my phone, but I think it was that weekend before the election."

"How did Rick hear that you'd been detained for questioning? He seemed to know you spent the night here last night. Did you call or text him?"

"No."

Conrad stood up. "Who did you tell?"

"Nobody!" Jeff slumped in his chair and shrugged. "Well, the guys at the quarry knew I had to come down to the station yesterday. I had to pull somebody in the office to cover for me, but I haven't talked to anybody else. I've been in a cell!" Jeff waved his arm out to his side. "How could I?"

"Okay. Okay, tell me about that Friday morning that Hobart's body was found. You were seen on Eagle Bay Road."

Jeff stared at the table and crossed his arms over his chest.

"Did you see Hobart?"

"No. I saw his truck parked in the lot when I drove by, but I didn't see him. I didn't look. I saw his truck and I kept going."

"Why were you out there?"

"Not for Hobart! I didn't know he was out there. I don't talk to Hobart anymore."

"That's not what I asked. Why were you out there?" Conrad pushed his chair under the table.

"I was just driving around."

"Are you sixteen?" Conrad rolled his eyes. "Who does that?"

" I do that sometimes when I need to think." Jeff glanced at Conrad and looked back at the blank notepad.

"I don't believe that. People that drive around to kill time or work out problems, they don't drive out of town five miles and then go down a road to nowhere. Eagle Bay Road is a dead end and there's nothing down there except a few houses, some docks and boat launch. Now, do you want to go back to the cell and wait while I go door to door to see who knows you? Because I can do that pretty quick. It'll only take a couple of hours."

Jeff slammed his elbow on the table and then lowered his forehead into his palm. "It didn't have anything to do with Hobart."

Conrad rubbed the back of his neck. "Okay." Conrad opened the interview room door.

"Wait! Can I go now?" Jeff pushed his chair back to stand.

"In a couple of hours." Conrad held his hand up. "You've got a statement to write and I've got to ring some doorbells on Eagle Bay Road. Maybe then I can release you. Maybe not. We'll see."

'No, wait. Just wait." Jeff motioned Conrad to come back to the table. "It's stupid. I didn't want to say, but I was driving out there to see if Emma Norton was at home. She lives close to the circle across from the boat launch."

"You know Emma?"

"Yeah, we went out a couple of times, but she's stopped returning my calls. I wanted to see if she was home and if maybe someone else was there." Jeff dropped his head. "I know it's stupid, but I don't know what I did. I thought things were good."

Conrad waved his hand dismissively. "Write it all up. I'll be back in to check on you in a bit." Conrad pulled the door shut and shook his head.

Officer Kimball was standing at the mirrored window. "You got more out of him in twenty minutes than the detective did all day yesterday."

Conrad smiled. "Spending the night here was probably what motivated him."

"And asking direct questions," Gwen said. "Snell spent all day trying to be his friend instead of cutting to the chase."

"Everybody has their own style and every interview is unique. I know Jeff, so I can talk to him differently than I could a stranger. Snell was trying to get a feel for him, I'm sure."

"Maybe." Gwen smirked.

"I'm going to grab some lunch. Keep an eye on him, will ya?"

"Sure, Chief."

"Thanks."

CHAPTER TWENTY-NINE

"Did you see the way he looked at me when we walked up?" Arlene's hands were clenched around the steering wheel and she glanced over at Cora in the passenger seat. "You could tell he didn't want us to go in Hobart's office."

"He was surprised to see you."

"I have every right to be there. I could go there and sit in that office all day every day if I wanted."

"Yes, you could," Cora said, calmly. "I'm sure he knows that. He just didn't anticipate having visitors today and maybe wanted to clean up the place first."

"Oh, the mess is always there. Hobart's office always looked like a bomb went off in it, but he could find every piece of paper he needed. The mess wasn't surprising. I was upset that Ted had been in there changing things around like he was taking over."

"I know." Cora sighed.

"He took down Hobart's pictures and stacked them in a chair. Did you see he had Hobart's hat on his head? I embroidered that logo on there myself. I wanted to snatch it off his head. And did you see that picture of Hobart winning that award that the governor gave him? He's always had that on the wall. He was so proud that day." Arlene squinted as if she felt a physical pain.

"I know it's hard to deal with all of these memories." Cora was struggling just watching Arlene manage her heartache.

"That picture of us with his sister, Beulah, and her husband, Jim -- That's our family picture. You know Hobart and I couldn't have children. Beulah and Jim lost a child and never had another. We were all we had. Beulah had been like a second mother to Hobart, and of course as she aged, the roles reversed. Jim died fifteen years ago and the three of us remained. We were family and I know Hobart didn't have that picture in a chair stacked with seed catalogs. He had that picture hanging on the wall right in front of him."

"Maybe Ted took them down because he was planning to bring them to you." Cora reached out to put her hand on the dashboard as Arlene took a turn too fast.

"Pfft, he was settling in and he couldn't look Hobart in the eye. Well, that's not going to happen."

"Arlene, take a deep breath. I know this was upsetting, but you don't want to do anything rash.

You need him to finish out the season for you and then you can have a talk with him."

"I don't think I have to wait that long. I'm going to talk with Mickey and see if he has the knowledge needed to finish out the season. I want to get an idea of whether he's interested in running things next year, so I can make a decision about the future. I just don't know if I want to have the farm hanging over my head, but I know I want Ted out of there."

"It's a lot of responsibility."

"Yes, and I don't know all the details. Hobart talked about the farm, but from a business angle, not the actual planting and daily care. I would have to trust a farm manager to know that and I don't know if I can trust anybody."

"Are you considering offering Mickey a trailer on that lot in Miriam's subdivision?"

Arlene pulled her car into the parking lot of City Hall and parked near the back. "I don't think so. No one needs to live at their job. I think I'll let Miriam buy it back. She offered a full refund. Maybe she knows she can get more money. I could list it for sale myself." Arlene put her forehead against the steering wheel. "There are just so many decisions to make."

Cora Mae released her seatbelt and reached over to pat Arlene's back. "None of these decisions must be made today. Put that out of your mind for now."

"It's just so much, Cora." Arlene leaned back. "Thank you so much for coming with me and listening to me rant. I just needed to vent a little."

"Oh, I understand perfectly." Cora smiled. "I do my share of that almost every day! Poor Amanda is stuck listening to much of it. I don't think they pay her enough!"

Arlene chuckled. "Oh, Cora." Arlene patted Cora's hand. "You've been such a help to me."

"I'm always here if you need me. Don't ever hesitate to call."

"The coroner's office left me a voice mail that they are releasing Hobart's body to the funeral home tomorrow. That's the next thing I have to do -- plan a funeral." Arlene sighed.

"They will guide you through all of it. I promise, it isn't as bad as you think. If you need company, just call me, and I'll go with you."

"Thank you, but you've done enough. I know you need to get back to work. I'll call you in a few days and let you know how things are going."

"You do that." Cora opened the car door. "Just one more piece of advice, Arlene. Don't make any quick decisions. Nothing is urgent anymore. Take it slow."

"I will, Cora Mae. Take care."

Cora waved as Arlene backed out of the parking lot and drove away.

Walking in the back door of City Hall, Cora saw Thomas Womack in the lobby. He had run uncontested for re-election, but there wasn't a council meeting scheduled, so she was surprised to see him.

"Congratulations, Thomas." Cora held out her hand to shake. "I don't think I've seen you since the election. Congratulations on your re-election."

"Thank you, Mayor. I'm happy to be returning for another four years."

"What brings you to City hall today?"

"The council wants to meet this afternoon. It's informal. We're just hashing out a few things about the vacancy."

"Hmm, okay. I didn't realize..."

"It's good to see you, Mayor."

"You too, Thomas."

Cora removed her coat and hung it on the coat tree behind Amanda's office door. "Amanda, did you know the council was meeting this afternoon? I just talked to Thomas Womack in the lobby. He said they are working on filling Hobart's vacancy."

"Laura just told me. She said Larry Langley was here and she was asking if he got to vote on filling the vacancy, and I told her I didn't know. He doesn't, does he? I mean, that doesn't seem right. He loses the election and then gets to vote on who gets it. That's crazy!"

"I hadn't thought about it, but that's a question for Ned Carey. I hope he was invited to this meeting. Usually he lets me know these things." Cora leaned forwarded and whispered, "On the sly."

"He'll probably try to convince them all that it should be him." Amanda huffed. "Just like I said before, the devil you know--"

"Is better than the one you do not. Yes, I know the saying. I hope we are worrying about nothing, but I'll see what I can find out."

§

"Knock. Knock." Detective Snell leaned around the corner of Conrad's office door and smiled. "You busy?"

"No, come on in. Any luck at the quarry today?"

"Two of the guys I needed were at work and the third was at home. I had to follow-up on a couple of stories, but they all have alibis for that Friday morning. I didn't find anything out of the ordinary."

"Wiggins is gone." Conrad glanced at his phone when it vibrated. Cora Mae sent a text that she would meet him at the restaurant at six o'clock.

"I saw that, and I read his statement. I think that's all wrapped up tight. Don't you? I stopped in the bakery, too."

"Following up on Kelly Vaughn?" Conrad sent Cora a quick reply.

"Yeah, the owner said she was there on time Friday morning. I didn't really expect to hear anything different. I just needed to rule her out."

Conrad nodded. "So, what's on the agenda next?"

"There's Rick Manning and the farm. If that runs dry, I say we head back to the spouse."

Conrad nodded again. He was running out of ideas, too.

"I'll see you tomorrow." Detective Snell gave an informal salute and turned to head out the side door.

"Yeah. See you tomorrow."

§

Cora Mae decided to leave the office a little early. She wanted to change clothes before meeting Conrad for dinner and Marmalade needed her dinner first. The day had been tiring, physically and emotionally, and she almost regretted making dinner plans, but a change of clothes might just energize her. Marmalade began meowing out her greeting the moment Cora Mae opened the door and rushed to get to the kitchen in the hope that she might be made priority. Cora relented and opened the pantry for cat food.

"It's not really dinnertime yet." Cora looked down at her old orange cat who was circling her feet and peering up at her innocently. "Since I'm going out to eat, I suppose you can eat a little early."

The melodic meows turned into desperate howls once the food was opened and Cora rushed to prepare the dish. "Settle down. I'm working as fast as I can. Boy, you are a demanding little girl."

Cora chuckled and stroked Marmalade's back as she began to eat.

Leaving Marmalade to eat, Cora went to her room to change. Her feet were aching from all the standing in Hobart's office and the walking back and forth to load the trunk and backseat with boxes of files, pictures, and knickknacks from Hobart's office. She wasn't used to manual labor. With winter setting in, it would only get worse and she needed to find a way to get some moderate exercise. She didn't like to walk when it was cold. Sitting on the side of the bed, she lifted up her feet and saw her ankles were swollen. Grabbing a bed pillow, she turned and put the pillow under her legs. Reclining back to rest, she closed her eyes and thought about Hobart's office.

The office had been messy. The desk was covered with stacks of paper and the drawers from the desk were full. There were signs that a filing system had been started for him, but once the drawers grew tight, he must have decided to use a system of stacks to organize his work. There were bills, orders, agricultural articles, and printed emails sprinkled everywhere. Arlene had taken all of it. She planned to sort it all out and see what she could learn of the farming business.

Ted Aldridge had stayed away from the office after Arlene had advised him of her plans to pack up Hobart's belongings. The rest of the workers were out in the field and only Ted remained, leaning against the opening to the storage building, and watching them as they carried boxes to the car. He never once offered to help and Arlene did not speak to him when she left. He just watched the car drive away.

Arlene had indicated that the dinner she shared with Ted had gone smoothly, yet the interaction today had been unsettling. Arlene had approached Ted when they arrived at the farm and both seemed awkward and defensive. Not at all like two people who had just spent a cordial evening together. Cora couldn't help but think that Arlene had not told her the whole story.

When Marmalade jumped on the bed to signal her dinner was over, Cora glanced at the clock. "Oh, I need to get moving." Jumping up, she changed her clothes quickly, combed her hair and put on some comfortable shoes.

"I won't be late," Cora said to Marmalade who was calmly cleaning her paws. Grabbing her jacket and purse, she scratched Marmalade's head. "Don't wait up."

CHAPTER THIRTY

"Sorry, I'm late." Conrad Harris slid into the semi-circle booth they frequented at the Old Thyme Italian Restaurant and huffed. "Briscoe had to eat dinner and get ready for his date tonight." Conrad laughed when Cora Mae's eyebrows shot up.

"Briscoe has a date?"

"Yeah. Gwen Kimball is switching to night shift tonight and she asked if Briscoe could ride along with her. He's quite taken with her and I think the feeling is mutual."

"Aw, how sweet. Has she handled a police dog before?" Cora smiled and nodded when the waitress placed a pot of hot water on the table for her tea.

"She did in Minnesota. It was a little different than Briscoe's training. The dog she used was trained for search and rescue, but she understands the basics, and I went over some things with her in case something comes up where Briscoe needs to work. I think it's mostly just for company while she patrols."

"Is he going to stay with her now?"

"No, I told her to leave him at the station when her shift ends. I'll go in early and give him breakfast. He can sleep in my office during the day. I don't plan to do it every day. We'll just see how it goes."

"So, what did you and Detective Snell accomplish today?" Cora stirred sugar into her tea and smiled when Conrad moaned.

"Not much. He went out to the quarry digging around aimlessly and I talked to Jeff Wiggins a little. It was another wasted day as far as I could tell."

"Did you get a chance to read those policies? Arlene told me that Rick Manning gave her wrong information. Charlie Elkins has straightened everything out, but I wonder if Rick intentionally misled her or whether he doesn't know what he's doing."

"The trust? Jeff Wiggins said Rick told him it was void. He told him he would get the money from that old policy."

"That sounds like a motive." Cora smirked. "It's not correct, though. Hobart changed the beneficiary to Arlene before he put it in the trust, so it's still hers, even though the trust dissolves."

"Could still be motive if he thought it were true. Jeff said Rick told Jeff's ex-wife, Twyla, about it.

That's Rick's sister and I guess Jeff must owe Twyla money."

"Back child support." Cora nodded. It was the town gossip.

"So, Twyla has motive, too."

"Hmm, I hadn't thought about that." Cora tapped her finger on the table. "You have a lot of suspects."

"Yeah, to something that may not even be a crime."

"Are you ready to order?" The waitress held up her pad and pen.

Cora grabbed the menu and quickly glanced over it while Conrad ordered.

Ordering her usual, the lasagna, she handed the menu to the waitress and waited for her to walk away.

"What do you mean it may not be a crime. Have you found something that makes you think it was an accident? I thought you said the coroner called it a suspicious death."

"They did. I've just been thinking. We may be worrying ourselves about this for nothing. It's very possible that Hobart just couldn't pull himself back up on that dock. It's harder than you think."

"That makes Larry's actions a bit more questionable." Cora shook her teaspoon at Conrad. "Larry could be held responsible for leaving him, for not helping him out after he's confessed to being the reason that he fell in to start with."

"He could. I don't know if they would charge him or not. I'm just saying it's a possibility."

"But he had contusions on his face and head."

"That could happen when he tried to pull himself out of the water. Hobart was a big guy, but he was almost seventy years old. That water was ice cold. When he fell in, I'm sure his body was shocked, and he could have experienced palpitations, arrhythmias in his heart. Maybe he couldn't find the strength to raise himself up. If you don't have a ladder or anything to put your feet against, you have no leverage. The dock might have struck his face when he slipped from trying to get up. It would explain the wood under his fingernails, too."

Cora tapped her fingers on the table. She had to admit it was a possibility.

"Of course, we have to rule everything else out. We still have unanswered questions." Conrad took a sip of water. "Tomorrow I think Snell is going to talk with Rick Manning and go out to the farm. We ran some background on the workers out there and we need to see if anybody was missing from work Friday morning."

"That's where I was today." Cora Mae leaned back and placed her napkin across her lap when the waitress brought their plates to the table. "Thank you, dear."

"Can I get you anything else?" The waitress smiled politely at each of them.

"No, thank you. We're fine." Conrad smiled and then turned to Cora Mae. "The farm? You were at the farm? What were you doing out there?"

"Riding shotgun." Cora blew on the steam rising from her baked lasagna and cut out a bite size piece to place on her fork. "Arlene asked me to tag along when she went to clean out Hobart's office."

"Did everything go okay?" Conrad frowned.

"We got the job done, but Ted Aldridge was not happy with the surprise visit and Arlene was extremely upset with the condition of Hobart's personal items. Pictures had been removed from the wall and stacked in a chair. I didn't see that any damage had been done. I'm sure Ted was just trying to make some room to work. The office was very messy, but it was strange that he would bother with pictures on the wall unless he was planning to replace them with something of his own. I think that's what upset Arlene the most. She felt like Ted was trying to take over and she's not ready to let go yet."

Conrad nodded as he chewed.

"It was harder on me than I'd like to admit, too!" Cora shook her head and sighed.

Conrad tilted his head and lines formed on his forehead. "It was hard on you?"

"I'm terribly out of shape. All that packing and toting things to the car. It was exhausting."

Conrad chuckled and took another bite of his Spaghetti Bolognese.

"It wasn't just that." Cora took a sip of her tea. "It was seeing the fresh grief. I know what she's feeling right now, but I've got that put away. You have to work at getting it tucked away neatly in a box that you put in the top of your closet." Cora sighed. "It takes months to do that, but once it's up there, you go on trying to live the life you have left without that person. As time passes, other boxes get put up in the top of the closet and push that box further back. It's just not something you want to open up again. Seeing what she's going through opens that old box again and makes me re-examine all the little things that are in there. It hurts my heart." Cora took a bite of her lasagna and looked around the restaurant.

Conrad dabbed his napkin in the corner of his mouth. "I know it has to be hard for you, but your experience is what makes your help invaluable to Arlene. She has someone to lean on and someone she can trust. She needs that now."

"Yes, she mentioned today that she felt like she couldn't trust anyone. After Rick Manning tried to lead her astray and Ted Aldridge acted like he wanted to help her, but she found out he was trying to get her to set up a trailer for him on Miriam's lot, she thinks everyone is trying to pull something over on her."

Conrad nodded.

"Oh, speaking of pulling something over on you, Larry Langley was in City hall today. They had a meeting on filling Hobart's seat on the council and Larry was invited to the meeting. That seems inappropriate to me. If you see Ned Carey in the bakery tomorrow morning when you go down for coffee, can you put a bug in his ear? He didn't even give me a heads up about the meeting, but I'm hoping he was invited. The council members need some legal guidance on this. They don't know what they're doing."

"You think they're just going to put Larry right back on the board?"

"I think there are several members that will try to do that."

"Let's just hope that he doesn't get appointed to the council and get arrested again when the county decides to charge him with negligent homicide." Conrad smiled. "Wouldn't that cause a ruckus?"

"That could bring the whole council into question since his appointment would be entirely their fault. They all have to face re-election, too. They need to be reminded that this selection will be something they may be held accountable for later." Cora held up her index finger. "Maybe that's a bug I need to put in their ear."

Conrad laughed. "Maybe it is."

CHAPTER THIRTY-ONE

"Good morning, Amanda."

"Morning, Mayor."

Cora Mae walked through Amanda's outer office and into her own. Amanda followed and leaned on her door frame as she plopped her purse down on her desk while she slipped off her coat. "It's rather chilly out there this morning. I had to stop by Violet Hoenigberg's house for a minute this morning and left my car running so the heater finally got warm, but I had to scrape the windshield this morning. It's my own fault. I shouldn't have left my car out last night. Anything exciting planned for today?"

"You have a meeting this afternoon with the lady that manages the traveling arts and craft show. You need to set a date for their display to come to the community center. It has to be a Saturday and she wanted the proceeds to go to a local charity."

"I can handle that. I was hoping to take it easy today. I'm still tired from all the work I did yesterday with Arlene. I'm glad it's Friday."

Amanda heard a noise and glanced over her shoulder. "Oh, excuse me."

Cora heard murmuring from the outer office and peeked around the door. There was a young man at Amanda's desk that she didn't recognize. Tossing her coat in a chair, Cora walked to her office door and the young man looked up.

"Mayor," Amanda said. "This is Aaron Vaughn. He is Kelly Goins' husband. You remember Kelly?"

"Yes. Hello, Mr. Vaughn. How can we help you?" Cora stepped toward Aaron and shook his hand.

"Uh, Ma'am. I just stopped in to get the paperwork to apply for a business license here in Spicetown." Aaron glanced several times between Amanda and Cora Mae, twisting his hat in his hands. His voice quavered with nerves and Amanda jumped up from her chair.

"Oh, yes. We have a packet made up for that. It has the application and all the applicable statutes with the fee schedule. It's all at the front desk. Let me show you." Amanda glanced at Cora before leading Mr. Vaughn to the lobby.

"Oh, my goodness," Cora whispered to herself. Rushing back to her office, she dug through her purse for her cell phone. Hitting Conrad's number in speed dial, she listened to it ring until the voice mail came on. Tapping the disconnect button, she called the police department.

"Spicetown Police Department. Can I help you?"

"Georgia? It's Cora Mae. Is the Chief in the office?"

"No, Mayor. He left about twenty minutes ago to go out to Hobart Emery's soybean farm. You might get him on his cell--"

"Thanks, Georgie. I'll try."

Cora grabbed her coat and rushed out the door just as Amanda was returning. "I've got to go. I'll be back."

§

"Good morning, Mr. Aldridge. I'm Detective Snell with the Sheriff's Department and I think you know Chief Harris."

"Yeah." Ted nodded at Conrad.

"Well, we don't want to take up too much of your time this morning, but we have a couple of questions."

"Okay." Ted sighed, seemingly disinterested in providing assistance. "What do you need?"

"You gave us a list of employees, which we appreciate. Going through that list, we realized that we needed to also find out if any of these employees were not at work on the Friday morning that Mr. Emery was found."

"Uh, I'd have to look at the records. I don't remember off hand." Ted lifted his hat and scratched his head. "Let me go take a look."

"Oh, and we also wanted to ask about former employees. Do you know of any disgruntled former employees? Anyone that was let go or maybe didn't get along well with Mr. Emery."

Ted huffed and then chuckled. "That'll be a long list. That'll be about everybody that's ever worked here. Hobart was a hard man to work for. I'm sure he's got a lot of enemies."

"Any help you can offer is appreciated."

"Let's go in the office." Ted pointed toward the office door and Detective Snell followed him. Conrad looked around the premises. Seeing no one else, he slowly followed Detective Snell and Ted Aldridge into the farm office but stopped in the doorway and leaned his back against the door frame. He wanted to see what was coming and what was going.

"How far back you want to go?" Ted fell back into the office chair. "We've got three years of records here and the older stuff is at Hobart's house."

"Three years seems ample." Detective Snell glanced at Conrad and nodded.

"And as for that Friday, hmm. I have to pull that up on the computer, so it'll take me a minute to get that going."

"We aren't in any hurry." Detective Snell glanced at Conrad and found a seat in the office.

Conrad paced back and forth outside the office door. Glancing at his phone, he saw a missed call from Cora and an email from the state laboratory. Clicking the email, he saw it was sent to Detective Snell with a copy to him and it said that the lab had isolated DNA from the handle of the wooden oar that was sent to them. The lab advised that suspect DNA could be sent to them for comparison. Conrad looked in the doorway at Detective Snell who was making small talk again with Ted Aldridge just as Cora Mae's car pulled up to the farm buildings.

Cora flew out of the car door and jogged up to the office.

Conrad leaned into the office and held up a finger to catch the detective's eye. "You might want to check your email."

Detective Snell nodded.

"Excuse me, gentlemen." Cora's head popped around the edge of the doorway. "I just need to borrow the Chief here for a minute -- Just some city business."

"Sure, Mayor." Detective Snell waved his hand and smiled.

Conrad frowned as Cora Mae waved her hands for him to follow her out near her car.

"What's going on? Something wrong?" Conrad squinted into the sun.

"It's the hat. I tried to reach you. It's the hat."

"I just saw I missed your call."

"It doesn't matter." Cora shook her head and whispered, "It's about the hat. I just realized."

"What?"

"You know I told you last night that Arlene was upset yesterday because Ted Aldridge had taken down pictures in the office."

"Yeah."

"Well, she also said that Ted was wearing Hobart's hat. He's got it on his head right now." Cora pointed toward the office.

"Yeah." Conrad nodded.

"Don't you see? It's not something all of the employees have. It's a one of a kind. She embroidered that picture on there and the words 'Emery Farms'. Hobart wore that thing every day. He had it on the night of the town hall."

Conrad kept nodding. "Yeah. Okay, well..."

Cora Mae poked her index finger into Conrad's chest. "Hobart would have had it on his head Friday morning when he fell into the lake. He wouldn't go fishing without his hat!"

Conrad stepped back. "I need to check with Larry Langley."

"The only way Ted Aldridge could have that hat right now is if he--"

"--was at the lake, too." Conrad finished Cora's sentence.

"Exactly!" Cora poked Conrad's chest once more for emphasis. "I'll check with Arlene, but I'm sure she'll tell me he left Friday morning with it on his head. You can check with Larry or maybe Hazel."

"Okay." Conrad opened Cora's car door.

"See you later." Cora slid into the driver's seat and started her car.

Conrad pushed the door shut and returned to the office. Curling his index finger toward him, he motioned for Detective Snell to step out of the office. They had a few things to discuss.

CHAPTER THIRTY-TWO

"Morning, Mayor. I've got exciting news." Amanda held her palms together under her chin

Cora chuckled. "That's the very best kind. I've got some exciting news of my own, Miss Morgan."

"Ooh, this is going to be a fun day." Amanda chuckled.

"Let me get my coat off and turn my computer on and you can start." Cora bustled into her office and stripped off her coat and scarf, tossing them on the coat tree behind the door. Pulling out her bottom desk drawer, she dropped her large satchel handbag into the drawer and pushed it shut before sliding into her office chair. Clicking the button on her monitor, she turned in her chair and folded her hands on her desk.

"Okay, let's hear your news. I'm ready."

Amanda sat down in the chair opposite Cora's desk and held up a piece of paper. "Sonjay Wilson stopped in this morning with the signed lease and deposit for the east side of Paprika Park."

Cora Mae gasped and then clapped her hands.

"You are going to get your farmer's market!" Amanda beamed.

"When does it start?"

"He asked for the lease to start March 1, but he said we'd have to wait and see what the weather is like. He wants to hold the market every Wednesday morning and Saturdays, if he can generate enough vendors to fill both days."

"That's wonderful. I'm so excited. I've tried to get someone to do this for over two years. I know it will be good for Spicetown."

"Should we make a press release?"

Cora crinkled her nose in thought. "I think maybe it should be Mr. Wilson's announcement to make. I will tell the City Council at the next meeting though, and I bet it leaks around town anyway. Having a newspaper is just a formality around here. Most people find things out in the wind."

"Or in the beauty shop," Amanda added with a smirk.

Cora Mae laughed. Amanda's mother, Louise, had always controlled the town gossip in her beauty shop and it was not usually appreciated by Amanda.

"Well, I can't wait. I just said yesterday that I needed to start taking better care of myself. I need to set up an exercise plan and start paying more attention to what I eat. Having a source of fresh locally grown produce will be wonderful. That was certainly great news."

"Okay," Amanda said rubbing her palms together. "What's your exciting news?"

"Hobart Emery's murderer has been caught!" Cora held both of her hands out. "He's in the county jail as we speak."

"Wow! Who is it?"

"Ted Aldridge. You probably don't know him. He's not from Spicetown, but he worked for Hobart at his farm."

"But I heard that Larry Langley pushed him in the lake and left him. Was this guy there at the lake, too?"

"Well, the Chief said that Ted Aldridge drove out there after Larry left the lake. He went down to the docks to find Hobart to talk to him. They had some trouble getting along, and Ted was trying to work out a deal with Hobart over a place to live. From what I gathered, Ted Aldridge laughed at Hobart when he found him in the lake, struggling to get up on the dock. Hobart told Ted to help him out, but they ended up arguing. Well, he hit him with one of the boat oars to keep him from climbing up and you can probably imagine the rest. I think Hobart was knocked unconscious..."

"And drowned? How horrible." Amanda shook her head. "My mom knows his wife. She said Mrs. Emery is really sweet."

"Yes, and it's an awful thing, but at least the murderer is caught now, and he will be held accountable."

"And you didn't even get involved!" Amanda sat up straight in surprise. "You haven't said a word about this investigation. At least you didn't have to worry yourself about everything this time. Isn't it nice that everything turned out okay?"

Cora Mae smiled.

"Morning, ladies." Conrad stood in Cora's doorway with a small white bag. "I just popped in to bring you a roll from the bakery and I talked to Ned Carey for you."

Amanda stood up to excuse herself, but Cora waved her back in her seat. "Thank you for the cinnamon roll," Cora said peeking into the little white bag. "I was just telling Amanda about Hobart."

"Yeah, Ted Aldridge is trying to cut a deal already. There's not much room to negotiate. They've got his fingerprints and his DNA on the oar, not to mention the hat on his head." Conrad chuckled. "He knows he's going down for this, so he's just trying to get the best terms he can."

"Arlene is very happy, but I know she was so frightened at the thought she had dinner with a murderer and had a murderer in her house."

"I don't blame her," Amanda said. "That's just creepy."

Conrad laughed. "I talked to Ned Carey this morning."

"Did you ask him about this council member vote? Amanda and I were both wondering about that. It just seems that Larry shouldn't have a vote." Cora shook her head.

"Ned said he wasn't invited to the meeting either, but they called him after the meeting with a bunch of questions. I guess they thought they didn't need anybody and started having meetings only to realize they don't know what they're doing." Conrad shook his head.

"I could have told them that to begin with." Cora Mae scowled.

"Ned says that Larry can't vote in this decision because it's effective January first and because it's his seat. The funny thing is that the council told Ned they don't think they need to make an announcement on it until January first."

Cora Mae smiled.

"Now, Ned said he told them." Conrad held up his hands. "He told them they had only thirty days, but they think Ned is wrong."

"What happens after thirty days?" Amanda asked.

Cora Mae's eyebrows danced up and down. "I get to make the selection to fill the council vacancy."

Amanda's eyes widened. "Oh my, now that's just even more exciting news."

Cora Mae laughed. "We are full to the brim today."

"So, who would you pick?" Amanda whispered, leaning forward conspiratorially.

"Yeah," Conrad said. "I'd like to know, too."

"Well, you both will find out!" Cora Mae clapped her hands together. "On day thirty-one."

Amanda sighed as Conrad moaned and Cora Mae giggled in delight.

∞

★ The Spicetown Star ★

No Winner in City Council Election

— Final election results released by the city of Spicetown show that 71% of voters elected Hobart Emery to represent them on the Spicetown City Council. As Mr. Emery cannot serve this term, a special election will be held next year to select a permanent council member.

The current council members may appoint a temporary council member to fill the vacancy until the special election can be held. Larry Langley will continue to hold the council seat until the end of the calendar year.

Thomas Womack ran unopposed and won reelection without contest. His new term will begin January 1st without interruption and he will participate (cont.)

Charges Filed in Election Antics

– Kelly Lynn Goins Vaughn, 23, Paxton, formerly of Spicetown, was charged with trespassing and property theft in connection with the unauthorized removal of election signs from the residential property of Mr. Dean Teggers.

A court date has been set for November 23rd.

Ohio State Election Results for Nov. 3

All polling places were open from 6:30 a.m. to 7:30 p.m. Eastern Time and the outcomes of the 2020 election cycle in Ohio stand to influence the state's redistricting

Dill 'The Devil You know" Eggs

6 hardboiled eggs

¼ cup Miracle Whip or mayonnaise

1 T dill pickle juice

3 T chopped dill pickle

2 tsp. fresh diced dill

½ t Dijon Mustard

Peel eggs and slice in half lengthwise.

Remove yolks. Mash and mix in all ingredients.

Spoon into egg white halves

Garnish with tiny pickle slices & paprika!

Refrigerate.

Blueberry Buckle

¼ c butter

1 c sugar

1 egg

2 c flour

2 tsp baking powder

½ tsp salt

½ milk

2 c blueberries

In square baking pan, melt butter while preheating oven to 375 degrees. Cream butter and sugar first, then add all other ingredients. Spread in baking pan and bake about 40 minutes at 375.

Brush with melted butter and sprinkle cinnamon sugar over the top once it is cooked.

Next in the Spicetown Mysteries!

Cons & Quinces

I'd love to hear from you!

Find me on Facebook, Goodreads, Twitter, Instagram, Bookbub, Pinterest, my blog, my website or join my email list for upcoming news!

www.SheriRichey.com

Please consider leaving a review!
It is extremely helpful to authors and to other readers. We all appreciate your feedback.

Thank you!

CPSIA information can be obtained
at www.ICGtesting.com
Printed in the USA
LVHW091101200421
685008LV00016B/178